# Mock & Grinda

## A Love that Defies the Odds

The Mother's Children, book 1.5

Morgan Tonkin

ISBN: 9798811941674

# Free to Roam, Free to Think, Free to Love

Even at Winter's steady plod, it wasn't long before they left the last village behind. Grinda sucked in a deep breath, her heart thundering. It was hard not to be excited in the open countryside, especially with the sky so blue, the sun so bright, with so much to explore and experience, and with Mock at her side—or at her back.

Smiling, she nestled back into him, gripping his muscular forearms as they held the reins. She smoothed her hands over them, tracing his ropey veins. Once, she could have done the same with his scars. Even now, her fingers wandered, expecting to find them. No more. Not after the Mother—or was it her daughter?—had healed him. His nails were still black with grime, though. She chuckled. No matter how hard he washed and how much she tried to help, he never seemed to get clean enough.

Grinda didn't mind. She liked him that way.

'Thinking good thoughts, I hope, *biala*,' he said.

'Just about when we first met.'

She smoothed her hands over his forearms again, remembering how she had gripped them hard, frightened of falling from his horse as they galloped away from her burning village. His horse. No. *Her* horse. Spirit. Her giant, black draft horse. It seemed so long ago when she'd feared his thundering hooves and his enormous size. She slumped a little, the thought of his death bringing a prickle of tears to her eyes.

A mountain. *He will be a mountain, Grinda.*

Gazing ahead at the tallest of the Windy Mountains, she smiled.

She felt Mock stiffen slightly. 'Not such good thoughts. Best to think about ahead, not behind.'

'I have few bad feelings now.'

'Still ...'

She rocked from side to side. 'My backside is getting sore. Shall we stop?'

While Winter grazed, Mock and Grinda sat together under the shade of a tree, knees touching as they drank from their water skins and ate the last of the berries they'd scavenged along the way. Grinda licked at her hands, turned blue from the juice. She could feel Mock watching, smiling. Brushing the hair away from her neck, he kissed her on the throat, down her neck, then pushed aside the top of her tunic as he continued along her shoulder.

Chuckling, she mashed her blue hand against his cheek. He jerked back with a grunt. Far from discouraged, he grinned, grabbed her wrist and began sucking at her fingers one by one.

Laughing, she tried to pull away. 'Stop it! That's disgusting!'

'You asked for it.'

Dipping his tongue into the middle of her palm, he lapped like a dog until Grinda was reduced to a fit of giggling. Finally he released her, pulling her into his lap as though she were little more than a child. Closing her eyes, Grinda leaned her head against his shoulder as he held her tight, feeling his heart beat and the warmth of his breath against her face. Her tunic itched. She wanted to remove it so badly, to have his skin pressed against her skin, to have her breasts pressed against his chest. He wore nothing except his *kinta*: the animal pelt skirt all his people wore. He rarely felt the heat. Grinda wasn't so tough, dressed in her thick tunic and skirts. She yawned. She was too comfortable. Too sleepy.

She felt him kiss her head, her ear. Opening her eyes, she gazed into his deep brown eyes with that ring of ochre around the edges. She touched his heavily stubbled cheek, then ran her fingers through his beard. She couldn't understand how she once thought it so disgusting. All men should have beards and long wavy hair. All men should have big gentle hands, soft deep eyes and dark brown skin. Even yellow teeth! As long as they smiled a lot. She wriggled against his pelvis. Not to mention a cock that wouldn't rest. Burying her face into his chest, she laughed.

All men should be like her big, brave Mock. Her best friend. Her lover. Her *barbarian*. It was strange to think how far they'd come in only two months: she, his victim; he, her predator. When she'd hated and feared him. Recalling that stolen kiss in the chapel so long ago, she could only shake her head in wonder. How ugly he'd been. How filthy and sickening and utterly horrifying.

3

How enormously things could change.

'Stop thinking, *biala*. The past is over.'

'Sorry.' She peered up at him impishly. How was it he always knew what she was thinking?

His soft, warm eyes smiled as he pressed his finger to her nose. 'I'll have to make you forget.'

Grabbing his finger, she raised an eyebrow. 'Is that so?'

'That's right.' Gently, he lowered her to the ground.

*

Careful to hold his weight away, Mock rested on his hip beside her. He still couldn't get over how small she was. Always, he had to be careful. He laid his hand against the mounds of her breasts, almost covering her whole chest with his broad palm. Her blue eyes shone as she watched him. Her golden hair gleamed in the sunlight. Her kissable pink lips pursed. She was barely a woman and yet she'd seen and done so much. Small and delicate she might be, but she'd faced more than many of his warrior brothers could ever hope to claim.

A remarkable woman—and all his.

She raised herself onto her elbows. 'Well? I'm waiting.'

Grinning, Mock pushed her down. He shook his head at her clothes. Annoying. Frustrating. Long, heavy skirt. Oversized tunic. So many layers. How could she be so cold when he was always so hot?

The tunic bunched up with a rustle as he slid his hands beneath. Already, her nipples were hard against the gentle rub of his fingers. She lifted her rump as he pulled down her skirt. He kissed her bellybutton, her hip, then pulled back, brushing the back of his hand gently along the length of her body, over her breasts, over her ribs, her hip and down her thigh. She shivered. Goose bumps erupted beneath his touch.

'Mock,' she croaked. 'I really want—*need*—you inside me.'

Mock could have laughed. A woman didn't know anything about need, not compared with a man. She couldn't know how hard the blood hammered in his veins, how fast his heart beat in his chest, how painfully his cock throbbed and his balls ached. Grimacing, he adjusted his *kinta*, then thought better of it and removed it entirely. His new belt of knives swiftly followed. Grinda's eyes glinted hungrily at the sight of him. Sitting up, she reached between his legs.

Mock grabbed her wrist. 'Patience, *biala*.'

Gently, he lowered her back down again. She gave a sigh but smiled. Kneeling in front of her, he parted her thighs, kissing them both on their soft inner sides. Her opening glistened, already wet. He laid a kiss there too and brushed a light finger along it. Sucking in a breath, Grinda shuddered.

How many times had he loved her? How many times had they held each other in the moonlight, in the sunlight, on crisp mornings and hot afternoons? Mock smiled. So many months lay before them. So many more moments like this.

'Mock!'

He gave a booming laugh. Sitting up, Grinda wrapped her arms around his waist and pulled him down.

They rolled in the autumn leaves as the sun glared above and the breeze swept through the branches, raining down a new shower of leaves. Laughter and shouting. She squealed and choked as he poked and prodded and tickled her. She was a blur of golden hair, of gleaming white skin and laughing eyes as they tumbled and played. Somehow he managed to get her tunic off, and, kneeling, pulled her into his arms so that her back arched and she dangled limply in his arms. She was trembling. She was so much in his power, so trusting. *Take me*, she was saying. Kissing her between her breasts, he lowered her to the ground.

Everything slowed as he entered her. She groaned as though it pained her, then groaned again, louder and more quickly as he thrust. Pressing his cheek against hers, he whispered *biala* into her ear, over and over. *Cherished one.* The love of his life. The mother of his future children. His best friend.

Then he was groaning along with her. Faster, he thrust, until the world was nothing but a blur and he felt nothing but the fire in his balls and Grinda's warm, sweet breath against his cheek.

Mock grunted, Grinda cried out and they wrapped their arms around each other. He rolled onto his side, pulling her along with him as he pressed his nose into the nape of her neck and took a deep breath. There, they stayed, as their bodies eased their throbbing and the heat between them slowly cooled. Looking up, he met her eyes and kissed her, long and deep, her lips soft against his, his tongue wet against hers.

Still connected. Deep inside. Hearts thudding in time.

So many months ahead.

He couldn't wait.

# A Pointy Challenge

'What are you doing?'

'Making a spear.'

His blade scraped against the wood, timber flakes curling in a pile at his feet. He'd cut down a long spindly tree and had been busy chopping and whittling for some time. It sat across his lap, already shaping into something smooth and even. The little forest crowded around them, their trunks flashing red against the flames. The moon peered down through the branches, yellow tonight.

Grinda licked the grease from her mouth, the taste of the fox she'd eaten still salty and thick on her lips.

'Do you need to?' she said. 'We've been eating well enough.'

'It's not enough for me, *biala*. And it shouldn't be enough for you. Not while you're with babe. I'll catch you real food.'

She instinctively touched her belly. Ten weeks, she thought, but couldn't be sure. The days and weeks and months were starting to roll into one. It was still too soon for a big appetite, though. She wasn't even showing yet. 'Like what?'

'Boar, deer, maybe even wolf.'

Her heart flipped. 'Wolf?'

He looked at her, eyes dark against the flames. 'Yes. The further we travel north, the thicker and older the forests become and the more predators. Fear not. I'll protect you. I killed my first wolf when I was still a boy.'

A long sliver of wood fluttered to the ground. She watched him quietly. It was hard work, she could see. The muscles in his upper arms bulged, his veins stood out, that long tendon in his neck was taut. He hadn't noticed but his *kinta* had ridden high up his thighs, giving her a very revealing view of his manhood. She licked her lips again.

'If you continue to look at me like that, *biala*, I'm going to cut myself.'

'Sorry.'

Eyes still on his work, he smiled. His hair trailed over his broad chest, looking almost red in the firelight. That masculine knot in his throat bobbed as he swallowed. And those fingers—so strong, so deft. Despite what he claimed, he would never cut himself.

She continued to watch him. Winter nickered in his sleep as he stood roped to a nearby tree, his head low, his white mane hanging around his big, flat head.

'Will you give me a try?' she asked.

'Try what?'

She nodded at the half-made spear. 'A throw.'

9

He peered at her in surprise. 'I suppose. But it may be too heavy for you.'

She straightened, fisting her hands around her knees. 'I might be small but I'm not that weak.'

Turning back to the spear, he gave a knowing smile, a deep, sultry groove in one cheek. 'If you wish it, *biala*. Anything you want.'

*

It was a good morning for a hunt, Grinda thought, though she hadn't actually hunted before so she couldn't be sure; a cloudless day with a gentle breeze.

Mock walked ahead, spear in hand. She studied it. It *did* look heavy and very long, much bigger than the one his barbarian brothers had left him when they'd expelled him from their camp.

They walked to the edge of the trees, then out into the open. Grinda squinted against the harsh blaze of light. Mock kept walking and she followed until they stood a considerable distance away from the woods.

He looked down at her, smiling that frustratingly knowing smile, as though he already knew she was going to fail.

Grinda lifted her chin. She would prove him wrong. 'I thought we were going to hunt? Shouldn't we go *deeper* into the forest?'

'Patience, *biala*. You haven't even thrown it yet. Practice first.'

Grinda pursed her lips.

'Now,' he said, hefting the spear onto his shoulder. 'Step away.' Facing the woods, he focused. Several moments passed before he took his first step. He was slow at first, taking long strides, before falling into a sprint. He pulled his arm back. The big muscles in his shoulder bunched; his neck corded. Then he released. Grinda's eyes widened as it soared high into the air. It was so fast she could hear it whistling. It arced, plateaued, then fell, lodging deep into a tree with a heavy thud that she felt through her feet.

Grinda stared. Mock's eyes glittered as he turned to her. 'Easy as that. Now, your turn.'

\*

They stood at the tree, Mock waiting patiently as Grinda tried to yank out the spear, or at least what he called a spear. It didn't have a proper point yet, merely his knife tied tightly to the end. Once he made his first real kill, he would shape and sharpen some bone instead.

He tried not to smile as she struggled. It was a good throw, even for him, particularly since the shaft had a curve to it which meant it didn't throw entirely straight. It required a lot of skill but luck as well, though he wouldn't tell Grinda that.

Finally, he felt pity, and made to grab it. 'Here, let me help.'

'No,' she gasped. 'I've got it.'

He stepped away. Bracing a foot against the trunk, she heaved, failed, then heaved again, finally wrenching it free. Surprised, she stumbled back, falling on her arse. Mock laughed. Grinda tossed her hair.

Standing awkwardly, she held the spear like she would a post, one end braced against the ground. It was taller than she was. He twisted his lips, trying not to smile.

Grinda nodded. 'Let's do it then.'

She tried to hold the spear in one hand as she walked, but it was too heavy, so cradled it against her chest with both her hands instead. Mock's heart lurched. He should have made a shorter, lighter spear. But how could he have predicted she would want to hunt? She'd never shown any interest before.

She kept walking, apparently determined to throw from where Mock had. He squeezed her shoulder, stopping her halfway. 'Far enough, *biala*.'

Turning to face the trees, she held her mouth tight and narrowed her eyes. Though she tried not to show it, he could see how she strained to raise the spear to her shoulder. It wobbled. The back of it hit the ground. She used her other hand to try and straighten it, only for the point to dip instead.

Finally, she dropped it with a hiss, shaking her hand at the strain in her wrist. He was about to make a joke when he saw the tears in her eyes. He picked up the spear.

'Here, *biala*,' he said gently. 'Let me help for now until you're ready.'

She said nothing and didn't resist, keeping her head lowered as she tried to hide her disappointment.

Helping her to hold it aloft, he shifted her hand further down the shaft. 'Try here. Now, spread your legs. Left foot forward and make sure you're evenly balanced.'

He stood close behind her, one hand on her hip, the other tightened around the hand gripping the shaft. 'Keep it steady. Now, just focus on throwing straight, not on power.'

She stared ahead.

'Take a few steps, then run, making sure to pull back as you do.'

She went for it and he followed, still helping to hold the spear aloft. She pulled back and released. It flew ... *thunk*. He raised his eyebrows: it had lodged into the base of the tree. Not deep, barely piercing the bark, but enough that it held for a few moments before falling to the ground. And more importantly, Grinda was smiling.

Brushing aside her hair, he pressed his lips to the nape of her neck. 'Good job, *biala*.'

She nodded. 'It's a start.' She turned, smiling up at him, as she placed her hands on his hips and drew him close. 'You're a patient teacher.'

He kissed her head. 'I'll make you a shorter, lighter one.'

'You don't have to do that.'

'Yes, I do. Then we can hunt together.'

Her smile turned doubtful. 'Do the Quarthi women hunt?'

'Some do.'

'Are they good?'

'Very good. But they learn as children. It takes years of practice.'

Lowering her eyes, she nodded. Curling an arm around her waist, he lifted her chin and kissed her. 'You did good.'

'Thanks to you.'

'Thanks to *us*.'

They smiled at each other.

# Nightmares

Grinda's breasts were pressed up against Mock's chest. Eyes closed, she felt him breathe: in and out, in and out. Slow and powerful, long and deep. Tucking her face into the curve of his throat, she snuggled in closer.

In and out. In and out. She breathed in time with him, heart beating slow against his. His arm was draped around her, limp and heavy with sleep. His cock pressed stickily against her, his hairs itching her legs. They'd made love twice that night and she could still feel the light brushing of his lips as he kissed her throat, the heaviness of his body upon hers, the heat of his seed as it trailed down her thigh.

He'd made a bedding of leaves and grass for them to lie in, soft and sweet smelling. Days before, he'd caught and killed a small bear and fashioned a pelt. More for her than for him; he rarely got cold. Though it was a cool night, the heat of him and of their lovemaking had made her fling it off so that they slept naked together beneath the canopy, the trees watching on, the moon gleaming against the sweat on their skin.

He didn't stir, even as she kissed his neck and slid a hand around his arse. He was like that. He had limitless stamina when it came to hunting and fighting but come a night of lovemaking and he slept like the dead. She loved him like this, not that she didn't love everything about him, but especially like this: vulnerable, peaceful.

In and out, in and out, he breathed. She could feel it through his whole body, a deep masculine rumble that made her skin prickle, that made her flush with heat. It seemed so long ago when she slept with her family in their one big bed, in their dark hut, the light breathing of her brothers and mother and the snoring of her father echoing around her. At a sudden pang of guilt, she pressed her lips to Mock's throat again, then pressed her nose against him, breathing him in. *Stop thinking.* Her eyelids fluttered. That deep, thick, male scent of his—it filled her up and made her swell. Comforting. It made her forget.

Soon, she fell asleep.

Grinda's heart hammered in her chest. The lake of tar— it was back. It surrounded her, sucking at her legs and filling the air with its rotting stench. And beyond that was the *Morgrar*, the ash and dust, that absolute nothing from horizon to horizon. Above, a wan moon shone a sickly dull yellow against the haze.

Not again. It was supposed to be over.

Her heart lurched as she spotted a figure in the distance. Just like the last time, he was facing away, but she would recognise that broad, muscular back anywhere, that long wavy hair blowing lightly in the wind. Naked and lost.

*No.* 'Mock!'

He dipped his head, then slowly turned. Her heart dropped. He was injured again: covered in blood, hunched over in pain, his face all swollen up. What was happening? He was supposed to be healed!

'Grinda?' he called back.

He began to move towards her.

'Stop!'

But he didn't listen and began to sink. Desperately, Grinda thrust her legs through the tar, trying to reach him—to no avail. She was firmly stuck, and Mock was disappearing! First his thighs, then his hips, his waist, his chest. Finally, he was nothing but a head, those beautiful dark eyes filled with despair.

Then he sank completely.


Grinda jerked awake with a gasp. Panting, she sat up, hand to her pounding heart. Was it a vision? Was it another vision! She looked at Mock lying beside her and her heart froze. He was so still, so pale, unmoving. Exactly like that lonely night at the ridge, with the leafless *wark* and the dying Spirit, when Mock had lain dead and everything had seemed so lost.

'Mock?' she croaked.

No response.

Tears rushed to her eyes. '*MOCK!*' Grabbing his shoulders, she shook him. '*MOCK! MOCK! MOCK!*'

\*

Mock sat up, hand flying to his waist where his belt of knives should have been, only to remember that he'd removed it to make love to Grinda. It lay beside him and he quickly snatched out a blade, then leapt into a defensive crouch, eyes on the dark forest, arm thrust protectively around Grinda.

'What is it?' he said, eyes flicking between the trees, from branch to branch, from root to canopy, between light and shadow. His ears pricked up for any sounds of the enemy or a stalking predator, but there was nothing. He spun around. More nothing. Finally, he looked at Grinda. She was pale and shaking, her face all screwed up. 'What's wrong? Did you see something?'

She shook her head. Then he saw her tears and realised. He lowered his blade.

Dropping her face into her hands, she gave a wracking sob.

Sheathing his knife, he gathered her into his arms, dropping to his backside as he pulled her into his lap. Gently, he rocked her, arms tight around her, as she wept and shuddered. He'd been wondering when it would happen. It was four weeks since that night, since the time he'd been captured and tortured. After all she'd been through, she hadn't cried, hadn't brooded and refused to speak about it, eyes locked firmly on their future ahead.

It had only been a matter of time.

'You were dead, Mock.'

'Yes, but not anymore.'

'But you could be again.'

He sighed. What was he to say to that? He kissed her on the head.

She wiped at her eyes. 'What if it was a vision?'

'It wasn't.'

'But how can you know?'

'Trust me. It *wasn't*.'

She looked at him, pressing her lips together. Mock, above all, knew what it was to suffer from past traumas, to have nightmares so real they left one shuddering in the night.

She laid her chin on his shoulder as he continued to rock her. He could feel her tears in his hair and pooling in the nape of his neck; her soft quivering. He pressed his lips to her cheek and jaw before kissing her neck. She sighed in his arms.

Closing his eyes, he kissed her shoulder, letting himself enjoy her softness, her warmth. Placing a hand on the small of her back, he traced his finger along the very top of her crack. She shivered—always so ticklish there—then giggled.

Her cheeks were streaked with tears, eyes red-rimmed but smiling. She ran her fingers along the stubble of his jawline and through his wiry beard. She pulled back with a laugh as he chomped playfully at her fingers.

Gripping her around the waist, he kissed her. She looped her arms around his neck, pushing in close. Her sweet scent filled his lungs. The little hairs on her arms brushed against his, making his skin tingle. Her nipples were soft and warm against his. Kissing her on the nose, he lowered her to the ground.

They rested there, her head on his shoulder, his arm curled around her waist, their legs entangled.

He pressed his lips to her head. 'Better now?'

She nodded. 'Much.'

'It's all right to grieve.'

'I know. Do you—do you have nightmares about it?'

'Sometimes, but I'm used to it. And it was only *my* death I had to deal with, not yours.'

She rolled onto her side, looking up at him. 'Do you fear it? My death?'

'I try not to think about it. But yes, every day.'

She snuggled in close until he could feel her lips press against his nipple. Soon her breathing turned long and deep while Mock stayed awake, gazing through the canopy to the stars twinkling brightly above.

# Rainstorm

*11th week of Grinda's pregnancy*

Grinda huddled under the pelt, bunched up close to Mock. It had been cloudy and windy all day and the night was no different. The bushes surrounding them bent and rustled, flattening against the blasting wind. There were few trees, and their branches creaked and groaned like old women. She shivered. They'd taken refuge behind a ridge in the hopes of cutting out much of the icy air. It had partly worked.

She winced at a drop of rain, then at another. She looked up. Dark, heavy clouds blackened the sky. It was so dark she could hardly see her hand in front of her face. She shivered as the spitting rain turned to a shower. She felt Mock stir beside her.

'*Biala?*' he said. 'You asleep?'

'No.'

'We should move.'

He slipped his hand into hers and they stood together. The pelt fell away and she began to shiver violently. The rain was blowing along with the wind now, a blast of water that wet through her tunic and turned her skirts damp. As usual, Mock seemed unaffected, warm against her side. He picked up the pelt, then pulled her closer to the ridge. The ground was hard and uncomfortable, rocks poking sharply into her backside as she sat, but at least it was dry. Wind whistled through the gaps in the rock.

'Stay here. I'll be right back.' Mock disappeared into the darkness.

She heard Winter nickering, followed by a small curse quickly lost to the wind as Mock struggled with something. Grinda watched anxiously, hands fisted in her lap, huddled beneath the pelt. By the time he returned with Winter and the rest of their belongings, the wind was howling.

'You all right, *biala*?' Mock said as he sat beside her.

'C-c-cold.'

Cupping her hands in his, he blew against them, then dragged her into his arms. He pulled back with a start. 'You're soaked.'

Quickly, he yanked off her tunic. Her skirts followed soon after. She sat naked in his lap, his warm arms around her as he rubbed her up and down and blew at her hands. His hair was soaked, sticking wetly to his shoulders. More water dripped from his beard. He kissed her on the cheek, on the back of her neck, then adjusted the pelt around them. It was wet on the outside but warm within. Soon, her shivering stopped.

And then it was nice. She'd never felt so comfortable with the rain and wind howling around her. His powerful heart thudded against her and even now she could feel his cock harden, pressing against her arse. She chuckled.

'What's so funny?' he said, a smile in his voice.

'You.'

He parted the hair from her neck and kissed her there again, his wet beard brushing against her shoulder. He shifted awkwardly beneath her. Grinda might be comfortable but Mock had to endure rocks in his backside.

'You're never going to sleep like this,' Grinda said guiltily.

He yawned. 'I'll sleep tomorrow.'

Winter stomped his hoof and nickered. The wind howled. The rain hammered. Nestling into the curve of Mock's body, Grinda closed her eyes.

*

Despite his discomfort, Mock did manage to fall asleep, though he dreamed that a hundred pixies armed with scythes were jabbing at his arse.

He shifted with a grunt. At least Grinda was comfortable, lying warm and limp in his lap, her head heavy against his shoulder. She was breathing deeply, her fingers twitching against his chest, breaths hot against his nipple.

Winter gave a snort, stomped, then whickered. Mock opened his eyes. He blinked, bleary-eyed. The rain was still pounding, the wind howling and it was so dark he was almost blind. But there was something different.

He squinted. Something was moving to and fro like a tide, and it was all around them. His eyes widened.

'Grinda.' He shook her.

She stirred. 'Wha'?'

'We have to go—*now*.'

He began climbing to his feet and she quickly pulled out of his lap in a panic. 'What's wrong? What's the matter?'

'Can you swim?'

She looked up at him, a shadow in the darkness, then looked around her. She sucked in a breath.

He grabbed her arm and squeezed. '*Can you swim?*'

She nodded.

They moved quickly as they loaded Winter with their supplies. By the time they were ready the water was already lapping at their toes.

'How did this happen?' Grinda shouted above the wind as they waded into the water. She gasped at the cold, then gave a little shriek, her hand squeezing Mock's. Behind them, Winter wasn't happy either, snorting and whinging as Mock pulled him along by the reins.

'My fault.' He should have known. It had been dark when they arrived and he'd been tired and careless and hadn't taken proper notice of the surrounding landscape. Looking back now, he could see it: the surrounding hills and ridges; the rocky ground bare of vegetation—they'd made camp in a shallow ravine. A boy's error.

Foolish. Stupid.

The water lapped at Mock's waist. It was almost at Grinda's breasts. Releasing her hand, he grabbed onto her upper arm for a firmer grip as the water churned and seethed around them. The muscles in his thighs hardened as he strained against its pull. One misstep and they would be sent careening down the river.

It was difficult. His body was numb and the water was creeping up quickly. It was almost to his chest now and to Grinda's neck. His heart was pounding. There was a rushing in his ears. *We aren't going to make it. We aren't going to make it. We* are *going to make it!* He could finally see the opposite bank—and it was just ahead.

The rushing in his ears turned to a roar. He looked towards the sound. Not in his ears—a *real* roar, so much louder than the howling wind. Surging, smashing, seething, a wall of dark water hurtled towards them. Grinda screamed. Mock only had time to seize onto her before it smashed into them.

Submerged. Eerily quiet. There was the gurgle and whoosh of tossing water as they tumbled and rolled and cartwheeled. Blackness. Blindness. They were completely at the Mother's mercy. Mock locked his arms and legs around Grinda, so tightly he thought he would strangle the air out of her, but he dared not loosen his grip.

*Don't let go.*

Something hard smashed into him and pain exploded in his shoulder. For a moment he blacked out, long enough for Grinda to slip from his grasp.

*No!*

He scrabbled for her, locked his hand onto something smooth and slippery, but a surge of water yanked her from his clutches again.

Lungs screaming, heart pounding, shoulder in agony, he thrashed towards what he thought might be the surface only to find more water. Up was down; left was right. There seemed no end to the Mother's fury.

More tumbling. Something grazed against his back. Something whacked against his thigh. His lungs clenched down, a breath away from filling with water. Another roll, a sudden thrust upwards, and his head broke through the surface. Air! Noise roared in his ears. Cold rain whipped against his face as he gulped and spluttered and gasped. Then he submerged again. All was silent, except for the gurgle of water, until he was thrust up again and he gasped down the air once more. His knees grazed against the bottom and Mock lurched face-first into shallow water.

Water swirled and lapped around him as he crawled along the bank. Only once completely away from the surging river did he collapse, chest heaving, sweet mouthfuls of air filling that agony in his chest. Rolling onto his back, he blinked up into the rain.

'Grinda!' He sat up and staggered to his feet. He looked around but it was still too dark to see much of anything. 'GRIIINDAAA!' He bent over, gasping, clutching at his chest and shoulder.

He paused at a sound, somehow holding his breath. He straightened. There it was again—a faint moan. How he heard it against the blasting rain was a miracle. 'Grinda! Answer me!'

Her cry was feeble: 'Mock.'

Relief swept over him. She was close.

He rushed over, limping and stumbling, his shoulder aching, his legs like water. 'Grinda!'

'Mock.'

Her dark figure was stretched out on the ground. He dropped to his knees beside her.

'Grinda.' He gently gripped her face. She moaned as he lifted her head. 'Are you hurt?'

'My head.' She touched his hand, her face, then just above her ear. He touched it too. It was sticky.

'Come on.' Sliding his arms under her, he heaved her into his embrace. Groaning, she clutched at her head.

Dizzy and weak, his shoulder a ball of agony, he staggered, but managed to carry her a safe distance away from the raging waters. By the time he laid her down amid a copse of trees, the rain had lessened to a sprinkle and the wind to a sharp, cold breeze. He could still hear the roar of the water as it surged and smashed and hissed through the ravine.

No shelter. No clothes. No dry kindling to make a fire. Their skin was wet against the icy breeze. Grinda shook violently in his arms, teeth chattering. Even Mock felt goose bumps erupt on his skin. With nothing else to do he held her close, rubbing her up and down, breathing his warm breath against her face, praying to the Mother for her protection, that Grinda's head wound wasn't worse than he thought.

Praying she would survive the night.

\*

Sunlight. Warmth against her skin. The day was so bright it made Grinda's eyes ache and her head throb. She rolled over with a hiss, grabbing at her head. Her heart thundered. All that water; tossing and tumbling, helpless in its grip, thinking she was going to die, imagining her lungs filling with water. Thinking she'd never see Mock again.

She shivered.

A big warm hand touched her shoulder. 'Finally awake, *biala*.'

She turned, saw Mock sitting beside her, then sprang into his arms, holding him tight, burying her face into his chest so she could breathe him in.

'You're all right,' she murmured.

He rested his chin on her head. 'In one piece. How are you feeling?'

She touched her head where she'd hit the rock. It was no longer sticky, her hair dry like the rest of her. She recalled hearing his gentle voice as she'd lain halfway between wake and sleep earlier that morning, when the world had been grey and she'd still been wet, cold and dazed. She'd felt his gentle touches as he explored her wound and washed the blood out of her hair and the mud from her body.

He smoothed the hair back from her ear, prodding her wound gently. 'It isn't so bad. Just a little knock.'

She winced. 'A little knock that hammers like the smithy. But what about you?' She touched his shoulder. It looked terrible: black and red and all swollen up. He was caked in mud from foot to throat. His eyes were red-rimmed, shadows beneath, cheeks drawn. Had he slept at all? 'Oh, *Mock*.'

'I'll live.'

She ran her fingers through his hair. Flecks of mud crumbled away. Somehow his beard was clean, looking almost fluffy. She smiled, then jerked straight, suddenly realising. 'Where's Winter?' Pulling out of his lap, she staggered to her feet.

'You shouldn't get up, *biala*.' He wrapped an arm around her waist to steady her as the world lurched. Dark spots clouded her vision. Taking her face, Mock looked into her eyes. 'Take deep breaths.'

Grabbing his arms, she focused. Her vision cleared. The world righted.

Hand in hand, they wandered back to their old camp. Mock must have lost his *kinta* in the water. She curled a hand around his backside.

When they broke through the trees, Grinda gasped. The water was gone, leaving a river of mud and debris in its wake. Even the ridge they'd been sleeping up against hadn't escaped the flood, submerged in mud and branches and a whole host of soggy things.

Then she saw him. She gave a cry.

'That bloody beast,' Mock smiled.

Winter was quietly grazing along the opposite back where the mud hadn't reached and where the grass was green and long. Caked in dried mud up to his belly, he was swishing his tail, looking perfectly content, as though nothing had happened.

Laughing, Grinda shook her head. He was like a rock or a heavy log, lazy and useless but completely unflappable. Their supplies were gone but she could see what might have been the sleeve of her tunic and the gleam of a blade in amongst the muddy debris. It was going to be a long morning retrieving it all.

'Where did you want to start?' Mock asked, already sounding tired at the thought.

'Later.'

'I said where, not when.'

Smiling, she pulled his arms around her, then gently cupped his balls. 'Right here.'

Mock laughed.

# Touches & Gazes, Eyes & Fingertips, Lips & Smiles

A man. *Her* man. The thought that something so wonderful could be hers baffled her. She looked back into his dark, gleaming eyes. They were so intense, possessive, hungry.

Grinda lowered her eyes as she dragged her fingertips lightly down his chest. It was hard to meet that gaze sometimes. It made her shiver, made her heart pound, made the blood rush into her cheeks, into her nipples and down into her hips until her whole body throbbed and thrummed and burned.

And when he touched her ...

She shivered again, her skin prickling into goose bumps as he brushed his fingers against the side of her right breast, then held her around the ribs, his hand so big against her it almost seemed there was more of him than her.

They were sitting opposite each other, legs crossed, shins pressed up against each other. They often did this, just touching and exploring. The flames of their little fire flickered against their naked skin, turning Grinda scarlet and Mock burnished copper. It wasn't so dark tonight; the moon coasted along a tide of white fluffy clouds.

His hand lowered, cupping her hip, as Grinda dragged her fingertips down his muscular abdomen and into his lap. He sucked in a breath as she touched him between the legs, then arched his neck with a groan that rumbled through his body as she wrapped her hand around him.

Though they'd barely known each other three months, it was hard to remember when Grinda hadn't known him. Had she ever been alone? Had she ever not known the warm heat of his hands, his gentle eyes, that smile that made her heart burst with excitement?

Had she ever been a virgin?

He gasped as she smoothed her hand along his length. How could something so hard be so velvety and soft? Up and down, up and down, she stroked him. He dropped his chin, watching her. His eyes were glittering now, almost predatory and *oh* so very very dark.

He released her hip, clenching both his hands around his knees instead. Veins bulged on the backs of them, up his forearms and across his chest. One throbbed in his temple. He began to tremble.

Grinda smiled. How could someone so big and strong be so completely within her power?

A warm droplet of seed trickled over her fingers. Her smile broadened, then she laughed, shattering the quiet of the woods, taunting him. He smiled too but it was dark and dangerous. How long could he last?

She leaned towards him, he met her halfway, and they kissed, soft and slow, their lips barely brushing, their tongues sweeping briefly against each other, though she knew how Mock must have been fighting to hold himself back.

Pulling away, she touched his hair, ran it through her fingers, then touched his knee and inner thigh before slowly walking her fingers towards his groin. Mock grunted and licked his lips, shifting as his cock engorged even more. It was red now. Scarlet. Thick and hard. Another bead of seed glistened at the tip.

He grunted again as she touched his balls. His ribs rippled beneath the muscles of his broad chest as he began to pant, then gasp. She stroked them, so soft and wrinkled in her hand. She winced. Not so long ago they were gone, nothing but a bloodied mess between his legs. Closing her eyes, she took a breath.

'*Biala.*'

She opened them again. He swallowed, gritted his teeth. The big tendon in his neck strained. Sweat beaded the hairs on his chest; more pooled in the creases of his abdomen.

No need for him to ask, to beg, to plead. She crawled into his lap.

\*

Mock released a breath, tried to suck in another but it caught in his throat. Her lower parts were soft and warm against him—and very wet. He touched her there —sopping. Clutching onto him, she gasped as he stroked her opening.

Then she shifted, and Mock settled his hands on her hips as she grabbed his cock and lifted herself. Her warm wetness brushed against his tip as she slowly eased herself over him. Soft, warm and slippery—she encompassed him. Sweat trickled down the side of his face. His heart hammered in his chest so hard he thought he was going to pass out. He tried not to dig his fingers into her hips as she gazed at him in that way, eyes bright and glittering. She gave a small hiss of discomfort as she took all of him inside her. He could feel the muscles of her channel tense around him. Even after all their lovemaking, he was still a tight fit.

Then she relaxed, smiling up at him, no doubt enjoying the look on his face. She liked torturing him, and he couldn't deny how he liked being tortured.

Grinda didn't move, brushing her hands slowly down his arms. Grabbing one of his hands, she kissed his palm, then tilted her face towards him and they locked lips. Still, she didn't move. Mock tried to focus on the softness of her mouth and the wetness of her tongue, rather than the warm, soft slipperiness of her womanhood.

Impossible.

He pulled away, panting, eyes burning in his head. His heart was knocking against his ribcage. All his muscles were tensed to breaking point. He couldn't breathe, couldn't think. The world had vanished: the clouds, the forest, the ground beneath. All he knew was the ache in his balls, the fire in his cock and that look in Grinda's eyes.

'*Biala.*' He swallowed, licked his lips. 'You're destroying me.'

Dragging her fingers through his beard, she finally began to rock. He pulled her against him with a grunt. It was beyond pain and pleasure now—a wild throbbing that burned through his body. He thrust his hips, and she cried out. Deep. Hard. Long. He thrust again. She arched her neck and he kissed her on that pulsing notch at her throat.

That burning became liquid. Molten. She cried out again as her whole body convulsed around him. The end was like a tide, a surge, a crashing wave. Crushing her against him, Mock shuddered. Throbbing. Aching. He shivered, shuddering again as he crushed her some more. Pulsing. And he couldn't tell whether it was him or her.

They might have been finished but he didn't let go, still holding her to his chest, feeling her heart hammering against him. There was still that wild throbbing but it was easing now. The sounds of their gasping filled the quiet of the night. Grinda didn't move, slumped against him, her breath hot in his ear, her skin warm and sticky against his. Brushing away her hair, Mock laid his lips against her neck, enjoying the feel of her, the smell of her, and he couldn't help but wonder if he liked this part more. After everything was done—being a part of each other.

Connected. United. One person.

Finally, Grinda pulled back, her breasts rising and falling and shining with sweat. Scarlet glowed in her cheeks. Her hair was tousled and damp, her lips swollen and red.

She had never looked so beautiful.

Gently, he gripped her neck with both his hands as he kissed her warmly, gently, achingly. Releasing her, he floated his hands over her shoulders, her breasts and gasping ribs, his eyes travelling over her curves as he did. He peered into their laps. Her thighs were clamped around his hips, her yellow thatch pressed hard up against his belly, and he imagined how he must look inside her. His cock gave a small throb at the thought.

'*Bial*,' she panted.

He looked up. '*Biala*.'

Smiling, they kissed again, hearts thudding, bodies aching, arms wrapped around each other.

As close as they could get.

Not letting go.

One forever.

# Sunset

*12th week of pregnancy*

Grinda pressed her lips around the *nuk* and took a slow, deep breath, letting the *chokra* turn her lungs hot, fill her veins and thrum along with the pounding of her heart. Ignoring the tickle in her throat, she focused on holding the smoke in. She would not cough because Mock laughed when she did.

'Even a child knows how to smoke *chokra* without sputtering,' he would smirk.

A long exhale and she leaned back against him, his chest warm and hard. A cloud of it wafted above them, the light from the setting sun cutting through it in scarlet streams. Mock's big hand grasped hers, encompassing her hand and the *nuk*.

'How old were you when you first smoked?' she asked.

'Not sure, but I was very small.'

Leaning over her shoulder, he raised the *nuk* to his lips, his hand still around hers. She felt the big muscles in his chest expand, then relax. Grinda smiled as she watched perfect rings of smoke float into the branches above. Purple, pink and yellow, the surrounding woods seemed to pulse and shimmer as the drug took effect. It was the beginning of the *gressa*, as Mock's people called a *shamri's* connection with the Mother.

'Mmm,' his deep voice rumbled in his throat as he relaxed back again, releasing her hand and the *nuk*.

Grinda half closed her eyes, enjoying the slow rise and fall of his chest and the feel of his warm breaths against her ear. Somewhere in the branches a bird chirped. She could hear the swish of Winter's tail, the rasp and rip of the grass as he grazed, even the slow, deep thud of his heartbeat. Then there was the whistle of air in his big lungs. Ants crawled and worms buried themselves in the soil by his hooves. In the branches above a squirrel worried at a nut, the scrape of its sharp teeth grating along her spine.

The woods had come alive. The *chokra* never disappointed.

Grinda smiled as Mock kissed her on the ear.

'Feel good?' he said.

'Mmm, definitely.'

Reaching under her tunic, he stroked at a nipple. His other hand followed, cupping her other breast. She laughed, then laughed some more. Resting her head on his shoulder, she arched her neck so he could kiss her throat, little wet kisses that made her giggle and shiver. She took another puff from the *nuk* and exhaled. Her giggling quickly turned to snorting as he reached beneath her skirts.

She looked up at him as he looked down at her. His eyes glittered. Then he leaned in for a kiss. A light brush of his lips against hers, a swift sweep of his tongue, and she stopped him.

Pulling back, she pressed a finger to his lips. 'You can't have me that easy.' Seized by a sudden rush of excitement, she slipped from his grasp and lurched to her feet. She grinned at him. 'Catch me if you can.'

Laughing, she half-staggered, half-ran through the woods, using the trees for balance as the ground rocked and rolled beneath her feet. She puffed at the *nuk* again. Her body felt numb. Her head buzzed. She heard the sound of Mock crashing through the trees behind her. By the sound of it, he was struggling as much as she was.

The colours of the *chokra* swirled and seethed around her, and that deep thudding seemed to reverberate through her bones. A branch snapped with a *crack*! and she squealed as a long, thick arm wrapped around her waist. Dropping the *nuk*, she struggled against him, trying to slip from his grip as he tugged at her tunic.

'You can't get away from me,' he growled into her neck.

She snorted. 'Mock!'

There was a cool rush of air as he yanked her tunic off. He scrabbled at her breasts as he kissed along her shoulder, his beard tickling her skin. He was panting, heart thudding against her back. Deep, hungry growls rumbled through his throat.

'Mock,' she gasped as he dragged his hands down her hips before gripping her between the legs. He tried tugging down her skirts but Grinda managed to slip away.

On the run again. She was puffing now, tripping over everything. The world seemed to list to the left, so that was where she ran, towards the setting sun, the reds and golds blazing like a raging fire through the branches.

Finally, her foot hooked around something, and with a grunt, she fell face-first into the leaves. Her body felt so heavy, the spinning world pressing her into the earth so she could hardly move.

There came the staggering thumps of Mock's approach, the crunch and crackle of crushed leaves. 'Grinda, you all right?'

She laughed.

With a heavy thud, he sagged beside her. Grinda didn't protest as he gathered her into his arms.

*

Her nipple was soft and salty in Mock's mouth. He swirled his tongue and she laughed and laughed to the point tears were coming out of her eyes. She was so drugged. Lying on top of her, he sucked at the nape of her neck, the spot she loved so much. Her laughter turned to squealing, which rang through the empty woods. It made his heart beat wildly. How he loved to hear her laugh.

Sitting up, he straddled her. He shook back his hair, then laid his hands against her hips. Slowly, he dragged his hands upwards, up along the slight swelling of her pregnant belly, then her belly button and ribs, until he cupped her breasts, her nipples sticky with his saliva.

She groaned, then laughed some more, her blue eyes shining, her cheeks wet with tears, as she grinned up at him. She had such white teeth between perfect, pink lips. He was about to kiss them when he stopped and turned his head. The light of the sunset blazed against his face. He paused. The hills ahead parted like a valley and he could see straight to the horizon. The sun was partway sunk, splashing the sky, the hills and the grass in halos of reds and golds and pinks. It reminded him so vividly of the world beyond the ether that he couldn't look away.

'Mock?' Grinda's little hand encircled his wrist. She smoothed it up his forearm. 'What's wrong?'

He looked down at her, then back at the horizon and all its startling colours, then back at her again. Pulling away, he took her hand and helped her to her feet.

She looked worried. Then he gently took her chin, turning her face towards the sunset. 'Look at that.'

Her eyes widened. She gasped. 'Oh, Mock. It's just like—'

'I know.'

He pulled her away from the trees and they sat together at the top of a small hill. Hand in hand, they watched. Beside him, Grinda sat quietly, smiling, a tear trickling down her cheek. Releasing her hand, he curled an arm around her waist and she leaned her head against his shoulder, her hand resting on his thigh.

Soon the golds, yellows and pinks were swallowed by a wave of scarlet that engulfed the plains, fields and half the sky. Beautiful. Conquering. Mock raised a hand against the glare, squinting.

'It feels like an eternity ago,' she said. 'Do you think we'll ever see it again? The world of the Mother, I mean?'

'You will, I think. As for me—unlikely.' He felt a rush of disappointment. He might have almost died there in the embrace of the Mother but he still appreciated the marvel of it. He hadn't forgotten the feel of something so powerful, so magical. The *shamri* were so fortunate. *Grinda* was so fortunate.

His eyes lowered to her belly. Overwhelmed by a sudden yearning, he touched it. Grinda blinked up at him, then laid her hand over his. 'She might not be mine by blood, Grinda, but she *is* my daughter, from now until I die.' He raised his eyes to hers. 'I'll love her, protect her, teach her everything I know. And she'll come to love me, so much that she'll never know the difference. This, I promise you.'

Brushing away more tears, she squeezed his hand. 'You don't need to promise me anything. I know.'

She raised her face, he lowered his, and they kissed, long and gentle, as the scarlet dimmed to purple, as the moon drifted and stars spilled across the sky.

In the darkness. In the light. Now and forever.

Mock wouldn't let them down.

# Waterfall

Winter's hooves snapped through the bracken. His long mane and tail tangled in bushes and branches, leaving a haze of white hair behind. Often the way was so tight his big round flank scraped against the trees on either side. The ground was uneven, sometimes sloping up, sometimes down, covered in rocks and tripping vines. And yet, nothing seemed to faze him. Grinda wished she could be the same.

'Come on, Mock. Tell me; where are we going?'

'Be patient, *biala*, you'll see.'

Grinda thinned her lips. Why couldn't he just tell her! She sighed, tugging at Winter's reins as he trotted behind her. Mock had seen the thick band of trees in the distance as they'd ridden Winter across the fields: a shadow against the white horizon. It had been along their way so they'd plodded towards it, and the closer they'd gotten, the more excited Mock had become.

'What is it?' she had asked him

Mock had grinned, squeezing her waist. 'You'll see, *biala*.'

Grinda shook her head as she followed his broad back through the thick woods. It was always "*you'll see, biala*". She grimaced. More and more she was getting angry and upset over silly little things.

'It's the baby,' Mock had once told her, smoothing his hand over her belly. 'They can sometimes send the mother a little funny. And remember, you're carrying a *shamri*.'

*Still*—she rubbed at her arms—she hated feeling this way.

Hurrying ahead, dragging Winter behind her, she caught up with Mock and seized his hand. Looking down on her, he smiled. 'Can you hear it?'

'Hear what?'

He paused, forcing her to stop beside him. 'Listen.'

Now she could hear it: a faint thudding in the distance.

She raised her eyebrows. 'The Mother?'

'Maybe.'

She sighed, and he laughed at her impatience.

They continued, and the further they journeyed, the louder the thudding became until it overwhelmed the crunch and crackle of Winter's heavy plod through the leaves.

'What is it?' But Mock wouldn't answer, just wearing that secretive smile. Whatever the sound was, it was pounding now. She could feel it vibrating through her feet.

The air thickened with moisture. Then they began to descend.

'Leave Winter here,' Mock shouted over the noise, taking the reins and looping them over a branch.

'What is it?' she shouted back.

But he only took her hand and pulled her along. Now there was a strange hissing sound alongside the pounding. The slope turned very steep and rocky. Mock managed to stay upright but Grinda wasn't so skilled, dropping to her arse so she could use her feet and hands to navigate the slippery descent.

She paused, seeing something strange through the branches.

'What is that?' But Mock couldn't hear her, too far ahead, the pounding now an explosive hammering.

Finally, she reached the bottom of the slope. Smiling at her, Mock held out his hand, she took it and he helped her to her feet. She stood beside him, aghast at what she saw.

'Beautiful, isn't it?'

Grinda didn't answer. *Couldn't* answer. It wasn't just beautiful; it was incredible, magnificent, startling. She looked up at him in disbelief. Laughing, he kissed her head.

So much water! So much power! The thunder of it turned the air misty. Spray, as high as the cliff was tall, hissed into the air. The water beneath churned and roiled, only to flow away into a stream so blue and calm she could see fish swimming beneath.

'What is it?'

'We Quarthi call it a *zama*—the Mother's Knuckle. But in your language it's called a waterfall.'

'It's wonderful.'

'You'll see many more when we reach my people.'

She shook her head. There was so much she had missed stuck in her village.

Mock began to unbelt his daggers.

'What are you doing?'

'Going for a jump.' He dropped his belt. Next went his *kinta*.

'A—a jump?' She craned her neck, gazing up at the top of the waterfall—the *zama*. She seized his wrist. 'You can't do that!'

He laughed. 'Yes, I can. Just watch.' He paused. 'You should join me.'

'Definitely not.' She wrapped her arms around his waist. 'And you can't.'

Gently, he disentangled her, his hands firm around her wrists. 'Keep calm, *biala*.'

Heart in her throat, she watched as he clambered over the rocks towards the pounding water, bare arse clenching and unclenching as he struggled for balance. His long dark hair flowed down his back. He took a moment to look up, and Grinda briefly admired the broadness of his shoulders and the hard cording of his neck. Then he began to climb, hand over hand, muscles bulging in his back, veins fat and ropey. It looked easy enough, but she could see the rocks were wet and slippery with moss and every new grip sent a sharp stab of fear in her guts.

46

One false move ...

Then he was at the top and Grinda released her breath. He peered over the edge, taking a few moments to study the water beneath. He looked at her and smiled.

He jumped.

'No!'

*

The rush of air blew back his hair and screamed through his ears. The coolness of the spray was like ice against his skin. With an explosion of noise and a surge of cold, he hit the water. He opened his eyes. It was deep, the rocks sharp beneath. All the noises of the world muffled to a dull murmur. The surface bubbled and roiled with white water. A few hard kicks and he shot towards Grinda as she watched anxiously from the surface. A fish darted away. Something squirmed along the bottom, sending a haze of dirt through the water. The water was so clear. Grinda was going to love it.

Another hard kick and he broke through the surface. Grinda screamed as he seized her around the waist and pulled her in. She squirmed in his arms as they sank to the bottom. He let her go and she swam back to the top, leaving a trail of bubbles behind. He followed.

He burst through the surface, flicking his hair back.

'Mock!' She gave him a shove, teeth chattering, so pale her lips were blue.

He pushed down on her shoulders. 'Keep under the water. It's warmer.'

'It's freezing! And now I'm going to have to dry out my clothes.' Angry again.

Grinning, he took her hand. 'Come on, I want to show you something.'

She pouted. 'I don't want to see it.'

Pulling her against his chest, he kissed her on the lips, gripping her so tightly she couldn't move. Using his lips and tongue, he nibbled and gnawed. Soon, she sagged in his arms, neck arched and breathless. He released her. She gazed up at him, breast heaving, face flushed, lips red and swollen. She didn't look so cold anymore.

'Come with me,' he said again.

He dragged her along. She squealed and bunched up against him as they entered the turbulent water. Taking her wrist, he dragged her hand under the *zama*. She laughed in surprise. He yanked her completely beneath until it pounded on her head. With a shriek she tried to pull away, only for Mock to pull her up against him. Silly, cute little *faqwa*. It wasn't that bad.

He pulled her through until the *zama* no longer hammered against them but echoed around them in a small cave.

Grinda looked around in wonder. 'Amazing!'

Mock brushed her wet hair away from her neck and kissed her on the throat. 'Anything for you, *biala*.'

She looked at him, eyes glittering, then laid her head against his chest as she gazed up at the curtain of white water. They lingered there for a while, listening to the pounding, holding each other.

'You should try it,' he finally said.

'Try what?'

'The jump.' Her eyes widened and he laughed. 'Thought you wouldn't.'

She took the bait: she pursed her lips, set her jaw. Pulling away from him, she passed through the *zama*. On the other side, she was a glittering dark blur. He watched as she looked up. Then she waded to the rocky bank. Mock quickly followed.

Climbing onto the nearest rock, she began stripping off, spreading her clothes against its warm surface to dry.

'Be careful, *biala*,' he called to her as she began to climb.

He made to follow but she turned back with a scowl. 'Don't need you, Mock. I can do this on my own. I've encountered much scarier things than a simple *zama*.'

Mock grinned.

Pushing himself away from the bank, he floated, enjoying the view of her beautiful body as she made the climb: slim smooth legs, tight little backside, that little triangle of golden hair, now brown in the wet. He felt his cock stiffen. Her wet hair stuck to her narrow shoulders and curled around her slim waist. It was getting long. Soon it would reach past her arse.

She reached the top. She turned to him, legs widened for balance as she stood near the edge. Folding her arms over her breasts, she gave him a proud little smirk.

Mock smirked back. 'What are you waiting for?'

She tried not to look scared, but her face paled as she peered over the edge. A haze of spray blurred her expression.

'Keep to the middle,' he called to her. She shuffled closer to the edge. 'Careful!'

Mock felt a stab of unease. For a moment he hoped she wouldn't do it.

Then she leapt, and with a small splash, vanished beneath the surface.

Mock swam to meet her, diving and pulling her into his arms. She wrapped her precious body around him and he kicked back towards the top. They broke through the surface together.

Grinda squealed, then screamed, then laughed. She punched the air. 'Let's do it again!'

Laughing along with her, Mock seized her face and kissed her. 'We shall, *biala*. Together.'

# Blood & Fear

**M**ock woke slowly, stretching gently against Grinda so he wouldn't wake her. He opened his eyes a crack. The sun was already beating down on their little deer-hide tent and it was warm inside. Grinda was wrapped up in their pelts but it was too hot for Mock and he was lying naked beside her.

It was often like this: late nights, late mornings, peaceful days in each other's arms. Grinda was on her side, facing him, her chin tucked to her chest, her golden hair cast over her face. Here an elbow, there a knee, poked out through the pelts. He followed her slender neck with his eyes until Mock found the milky white softness of her cleavage peering up at him. Licking his lips, he lifted up her pelts and pressed up against her hot skin. He paused as she stirred, but she didn't waken.

Gently, he explored, dragging his finger lightly over the swell of her arse, along her crack, before smoothing his hand along the dip of her waist. Brushing the stray hairs from her shoulder, he kissed her neck before wrapping his big hand around her pointed hip.

There, he gazed at her as he felt the gentle rise and full of her breasts against him. Pulling back a little, he lightly pressed his hand up against one of them, her nipple soft and warm against his palm. He wondered whether she realised how much fuller her breasts had become. She hadn't spoken about it. They looked different too: the little lumps around her nipples were bumpier, the pink darker. He lightly pinched the tip, then slid his hand down to the swelling of her belly. Women were amazing: what they could do, how their bodies changed. As a boy, he remembered watching the women in his village with astonishment. He remembered watching Danna the same way.

He reached lower, to the coarse hairs of her womanhood, brushing his fingers through them. He parted her lower lips. It was warm, sticky and wet from their lovemaking. He eased a finger inside her.

Grinda stirred again and this time she did waken. She chuckled. 'Mock. You're naughty.'

Mock bit down on his lip as she grabbed his cock and squeezed. 'You can talk.'

She smiled, her blue eyes gleaming brightly between her heavy eyelids. He pulled his finger out, cuddled in close, then brushed at her cheek.

He froze.

Grinda kissed him on the lips. 'What's wrong?'

'You feeling all right, *biala*?'

She snuggled into him, so her lips pressed up against his neck. 'I feel perfect.'

He stared at the blood on his finger, then slowly pulled away.

Grinda sat up alongside him, the pelts slipping from her shoulders.

'Don't be alarmed.'

He pulled away the pelt from across her lap. She sucked in a breath. 'What's wrong? What's happening?'

'Don't panic, *biala*.' He grabbed her arm but the sight of more blood on his hand only made things worse.

Her eyes widened, then she paled. Her chest rose and fell rapidly as she panted.

He grabbed her shoulders. 'Breathe, Grinda. It'll be all right.'

\*

But how could it be? She clutched onto Mock as his face blurred behind a wall of tears. How could this be? Her daughter was special, a *shamri*. She had connected with the Mother. Big things lay in her future. Grinda knew it.

Mock wrapped his arms around her as she shuddered against him. He rubbed his hand up and down her back but she hardly felt it. Fourteen weeks. She'd been keeping close count. She couldn't believe it. Grinda had seen her daughter down beyond the ether: her long dark hair, her soft brown skin; those eyes. She hadn't forgotten.

She couldn't die.

The shuddering stopped. The tears slowed. She looked up at Mock, who was watching her sadly. 'This can't be right,' she said. 'We know she's going to live. We've *both* seen it.'

'That's right.'

She looked into her lap. There wasn't a great deal of blood, only smears along her thighs and no clots. She pressed her hand to her belly. And no pain. She remembered other women in her village in the same situation. Bleeding often led to miscarriage but not always. Some even bled the whole way through their pregnancy. She took a breath, letting herself relax.

'Everything's going to be all right,' she said. '*She's* going to be all right.'

Mock kissed her on the head. 'I know it.'

She looked around the little tent Mock had made for them: made of deer hide, big enough to crouch in, warm earthen floor. The last week had turned freezing. And the nights—not even Mock's body heat had been enough. But the tent was so warm, warmer than even her family hut back at Quay.

The Quarthi were so remarkable. *Mock* was so remarkable.

Mock pressed his forehead against hers. 'Wait here.'

'Where you going?' she said as he left the tent. He was wearing nothing but his *kinta*, his long hair draped messily over his shoulders.

Grinda wrapped herself up in their pelts, listening to whatever he was doing outside. Every now and then she would touch herself between the legs and a new tear would trickle down her cheek.

She heard the crackle of a fire, then the crunch of footsteps as Mock left to go somewhere. He returned minutes later. She heard him sit. Finally, she couldn't stand the loneliness. She got dressed, then crawled outside. 'What are you doing?'

He patted the spot beside him. 'Come sit, *biala*.'

She did so, watching as their only pot steamed over the flames. She glanced inside to find only water. 'Cooking something?'

Smiling, he dipped a finger inside, checking its temperature, then pulled the pot off its little stand. 'Lift up your skirts.'

'Why?'

His dark, gentle eyes waited. She did so, glancing briefly at the red splash on her thighs before quickly turning away. He tried to open her legs. She snapped them shut.

'*Biala*.'

She looked at him, at the tenderness in his face, then looked away again, trying to relax as he spread them. He dipped a cloth in the water. She gasped as he washed her, his touch light and gentle, the water so warm it sent a pleasant shiver up her spine. For a while she couldn't look at him, listening to his steady breathing, to the squeeze and dribble as he wrung out the cloth, to the light gurgle of water as he dunked it back into the pot, again and again. It took all she had not to pull away. Even after all their lovemaking, she had never experienced something so intimate. Something so private.

Eventually she turned to him. 'You don't need to do that.'

'I want to.'

'Aren't you disgusted?'

He didn't look at her as he spread open her woman's lips and cleaned deeper. 'Disgusted?'

'Men think women's problems are disgusting.'

'Not Quarthi men. Not *real* men. And certainly not me.'

'Sometimes my father made me sleep outside with the chickens during my bleeding time. Said I was too dirty. Mama had to too.'

Mock spat on the ground. '*Faqwa*.' He looked up at her. His eyes were glinting. 'We Quarthi celebrate a woman's first blood and every time thereafter. We don't fear it. We aren't disgusted by it. Our people cannot survive without a woman's moontime. *Faqwa*.' He spat again. 'They ruin their women.'

She paused, watching as he went back to his task. 'And what about miscarriage?'

He didn't answer. Finishing up, he patted her dry. After taking a moment to clean his hands, he took her chin. Grinda dropped her gaze. Her lips wouldn't stop trembling. He pulled her into his arms. Pressed up against his warm chest, she clung to him.

Mock didn't say a word as her tears burst free, only held her more tightly.

# Warks & Breaks, Mystery & Magic

*17th week of pregnancy*

L ooking down at herself, Grinda smoothed her hands over her growing belly. She was showing a lot more now, looking like a real pregnant woman. She shifted her weight from leg to leg as she stood at the cliff edge, waiting for Mock's return. She was starting to ache more in various places, and it was getting harder and harder to stand for any significant amount of time.

After that scare a few weeks back, she hadn't had any more bleeding. From what she could see, her daughter was fine. Though Grinda would have liked to have felt her kicking, just to be sure. The thought that she might be sick or hurt inside was a constant worry.

She sat, dangling her legs over the edge as she gazed into the distance. They were deep into the east now, where the open fields were few and the forests were sprawling and thick. She liked it. It felt comfortable, like home—if she'd ever really known such a thing. She laid her hand on her belly. It was because of her daughter that Grinda was becoming more and more aware of the life around her: the animals, the streams and *zamas*, the rocks and little lifeforms ... the *warks*. She glanced over her shoulder towards the woods behind her. There was one close by. She could sense it. There was no need for *chokra* anymore: her daughter was too powerful for that, even when so young.

My daughter—a *shamri*. A witch. The thought made her smile.

She looked back ahead. *Mock*. She sensed him now but couldn't see him. She lifted her hand against the glare of the setting sun, but the thickness of the woods kept him hidden. With the thought of meeting him down below, she stood, only to freeze when she felt something shift beneath her feet. There was a shudder, a loud *crack!* Then her feet were sinking. She only had time to suck in a breath before she fell.

Time slowed as the cool evening air slapped against her face and the ground came up to meet her. It wasn't a high drop but the ground knocked the wind out of her, nonetheless. She tumbled over and over. Pain seared through her shoulder and through her hip. Her nose crunched. Then she stopped. Sprawled on her back, she squinted into the red sky, unable to move or think. Her ears rang. Something warm and wet trickled down the side of her head. She winced at a sting as she wiped it away. There was blood on her fingers and on her tunic.

She sat up with a start, grabbed at her shoulder, then at her hip with a hiss. But she quickly forgot about the pain as she lifted up her torn tunic and frantically checked herself. Except for a long, bleeding graze down the side of her belly, there didn't seem to be any damage. She touched her belly all over, bracing herself for the worst. No pain. No pain. No pain. She took a shuddering breath, then glanced behind her. The top of the little cliff had given away, and she was sitting in a river of rocks and debris. She dropped her head into her hands.

Slowly, she eased herself to her feet, leaning on her right leg with a wince. There was no way she was going to try and climb back up. She would have to go around —and quickly. The last thing she wanted was for Mock to get back before she did and worry about her.

It didn't take long but it was agony. She kept her arm tight against her chest so her shoulder wouldn't burn, and she limped at every step. By the time she returned to their tent, she was panting. At least she'd returned in time. She had hoped to wash off the dirt and blood before Mock got back but had only managed to wet her face by the time he arrived.

They stared at each other: Grinda's face still smeared in pink blood; Mock mounted on Winter, face frozen, hands twisted hard around the reins. He frowned, eyes trailing over the dirt and dust on her ripped tunic, her sore arm, her torn skirts and twisted leg, before turning to the now jagged and broken cliff edge. Nothing got past Mock. Tightening his jaw, he dismounted.

*

'Foolish mistake,' she told him before he could speak.

Crouching in front of her, Mock took her chin, gently twisting her head from side to side. A cut upper lip, a graze down her face, a swollen nose. 'You fell?' She nodded. 'I told you—'

'—to keep away from the edge.' She nodded again, then looked away, swallowing hard.

'Your arm.' She was holding it tightly to her chest. He touched it, then tried to move it, only for Grinda to hiss in pain.

She gritted her teeth. 'Leave it. It doesn't matter.' She lowered her good hand to her belly and raised her eyes to his. 'You think she's all right?'

'Any pain?' He pressed her lightly around the abdomen. Grinda shook her head. 'I'm sure she's fine.'

Her eyes shone with tears. 'I'm a terrible mother.'

'It was an accident, Grinda.'

'It doesn't matter.'

Shaking his head, he tried to pull away her arm again. There was swelling and deep bruising around the elbow. He winced as he slowly turned it over: bone was sticking out.

Grinda was looking away, unable to watch. 'Is it all right?'

'It's not good, *biala.*' Mock tightened his mouth. A break like that could kill a man, from infection, shock and a whole host of fatal things. If they were with his people, with the *shamri*, maybe something could be done. They could heal. They had poultices and wrappings that could keep the wound clean. But they were far away.

Grinda dared to look, sucked in a breath, then met his gaze. 'I'm sorry. I've made a mess of things.'

'No.' Grabbing her fiercely around the neck, he glared into her eyes. 'We'll find a solution.'

Biting her lip, she nodded, though he could see the despair in her eyes. She dropped her gaze, pressing a hand to her belly. 'I know a way.'

Mock pulled back, sitting on his knees. 'Do you think it'll work?'

Her eyes glinted. 'She healed you, didn't she?'

Hope flared in his chest. 'That she did.'

Grinda reached over and Mock took her hand, entwining their fingers. 'This is far from the end,' she told him.

Mock watched, his heart in his throat, as Grinda disappeared into the trees. According to Grinda there was a *wark* close by, within a half day's walk. A long way to go for an injured, pregnant woman, even one as strong as Grinda. He'd wanted to go with her but she'd been adamant that she needed to go alone.

Mock paced the ground in front of the tent until the grass turned to dirt and hardened into clay. The fire burned down. The last, lingering smell of the *chokra* had blown away on the breeze hours before. The drug had helped with Grinda's pain before she'd set out. Mock refused to take any, even if it did make the waiting more bearable. Sunset. If she did not return by sunset, he would go looking for her. He needed his mind clear, his senses sharp.

The sun descended and Mock wiped the sweat from his forehead, the muscles of his shoulders bunched tightly around his neck. He shouldn't have let her go alone. What if the splint he'd made her failed? What if she tripped and fell? He should have made her see reason. He should have forced her to take him with her. Sometimes he wondered at her strange choices and at his own weakness at letting her do what she thought best. He was the man, after all. *He* was supposed to protect her.

Sweeping his hair from his back, he tied it into a knot, only to untie it again, so he could rip his fingers through its lengths. He paced faster, his eyes forever pinned to the trees ahead, waiting and waiting, sweating, his guts twisting tighter and tighter.

Finally, he could take no more. Before the sun touched the horizon, he strapped on his belt of knives, sheathed his sword and stepped into the darkness of the woods. He fell into a fast jog, his heart pounding against his ribcage, the trees passing by in a blur of light and shadow. He could see her trail: the lightly crushed earth, the crumpled leaves and snapped sticks, the occasional strand of golden hair caught on a branch. Small things that only a trained hunter would notice.

He hadn't gone far when he heard something. He drew his sword, ears pricking up at the gentle crunch of ground litter. It was just ahead, heading towards him. And close. It had to be an animal. Although ...

He let himself hope. 'Grinda?'

'Mock?' came her faint voice.

Sheathing his sword, he sped through the trees. A short sprint later and he found her: a small dark figure, sunlight glinting against the top of her golden head. '*Biala.*' Her eyes, her smile—it was as though he hadn't seen her for days. His first thought was to sweep her into his embrace and squeeze her until she squirmed. His second thought was her arm. He slowed, then stopped. The splint was gone.

'Is it ...?' he began.

She smiled, then waved her arm in the air.

Mock grinned, and she squealed as he yanked her against him, hoisting her off her feet as he kissed her down the neck, smelling her, tasting her, taking deep breaths of her hair.

Grinda clung to him, legs and arms wrapped around him, face buried in his chest. Then Mock hoisted her properly into his arms and kissed her so long and hard she had to pull away.

'Mock,' she gasped.

Hoisting her more securely against him, Mock carried her back, kissing her along the way.

# The Easy Way & The Hard Way

Grinda closed her eyes with a smile. 'Can you feel her?'

Mock smoothed his hand over her belly. At twenty weeks she was getting big, probably too big. It worried Mock sometimes. The baby's father had been big compared with Paleskin men but not compared with Mock. Would it be safe for Grinda to carry Mock's children when it came time?

'Here.' Smiling up at him with her soft pink lips, she took his hand and pressed it just below her navel.

Mock waited, gazing at the white nub of her belly button. It had popped out the week before. The sight of it made him warm in the chest. It was cute. Grinda was cute.

He raised his eyes to hers. 'I can't feel her, *biala*.'

'Shhhh. Just wait. Close your eyes.'

He did and again he waited. Nothing. He was just about to pull away when he felt the smallest nudge. He opened his eyes with a start. Grinda laughed. And it wasn't just an ordinary laugh (though he had never thought any of Grinda's laughs ordinary); this was something different. She arched her long, smooth neck. Her hair flared around her like a halo. Her eyes shone. Her sweet voice seemed to ring in the air like a bell. She glowed. She shone. His shining star.

Quickly that warmth in his chest turned to a burn that dropped into the pit of his belly. Seized by a sudden, overwhelming need to have her, he slid his hand down to her hip, leaned in and grabbed those soft pink lips with his own. Her laughter snapped off. Her smooth, soft hands cradled his neck. The taste of her, the feel of her, the smell of her sweet breaths ...

*Ahhh.*

Somehow she ended up stretched out on the soft grass, though he couldn't remember pulling her beneath him. The warm autumn sun beat against his back. A soft breeze ran its cool fingers through his fringe. Grinda's skin broke out into goose bumps. He could feel them beneath his fingertips; from the cold or from her desire, he couldn't tell.

Her breasts were soft beneath his hands, her neck smooth beneath his lips. He slid up her skirts and felt the warm wetness of her womanhood. Sliding his hand around the back of her, he grabbed her round arse as he nudged at her opening with his cock. Wet and soft, she encased him. He pressed his lips to her shoulder, on that seductive notch at the base of her throat, then at the corner of her jaw where he let them linger, sucking her deeply.

She always tasted so good.

She had her eyes closed now and the sight of the strain on her face made him burn harder. Her lips pulled back as she gritted her teeth. Her body tensed. Her arms squeezed him hard. Then she shuddered. And as she arched her neck, Mock moved from her jaw to suck at her throat.

Then they were still, panting against each other's cheeks, arms locked around each other as the last of their pleasure ebbed away.

Kissing her on the corner of her mouth, Mock rolled onto his back, pulling her on top. Grinda lay there for a long time, unmoving, quiet. Mock closed his eyes, enjoying how her body rose and fell at every breath, how her heart fluttered against his.

Then he began gently rubbing her, smoothing his hands up and down her back, across the points of her shoulder blades, then down her sides, feeling the sides of her breasts, the points of her hips before following the curve of her arse and holding her there.

*

Grinda sighed. 'You have such warm hands.'

'Mmm.'

She ran her fingers through the coarse dark hairs on his chest, then glided the tip of her finger around his right nipple. It hardened. Leaning over, she sucked it between her lips. He gave a surprised gasp, then gripped the back of her head. His deep voice rumbled in his throat as he chuckled.

Lifting her face, Grinda leaned her chin against his hard chest, giving him a mischievous smile as she studied him. He was so handsome and the smell of him made her mouth water. Mock smiled, bracing his hands behind his head so he could watch her too.

Warmth spread up her spine. 'I love you, *bial.*'

'I love you too.'

'I don't ever want this to end.' She pressed her lips against his sternum.

'It won't.'

She kissed his other nipple, then laid her cheek against him with a sigh. Closing her eyes, she listened to the slow thud of his heartbeat. She shivered, no longer so warm as the cool autumn breeze dried the sweat on her skin.

Mock wrapped his arms around her in an attempt to warm her, then rolled onto his side, pulling her into his chest as he curved his big body around hers protectively. Soon, she stopped shivering.

Pressing her face into his chest, she took deep breaths, then reached for his hand, entwining his fingers with hers.

'Something on your mind, *biala?*'

'No.' She looked up at him. 'Why do you think that?'

'You're quiet.'

'So are you.' She smiled. 'I'm just enjoying how you feel against me.' Releasing his hand, she reached between his legs.

He laughed. He was sticky: soft and warm and sticky. Grinning, he grabbed at her breast, smoothing his thumb over her nipple. She shivered. She was getting so sensitive there now. Poking her tongue at him, she grabbed his balls. His mouth twisted; a fire lit in his eyes. Grinda squealed as he rolled her beneath him. She squealed again, trying helplessly to thrust him away as he kissed her all over: her throat, shoulders, breasts, hips, then finally below.

He peered at her from between her thighs. 'So you think you can get the better of me, *biala*.' She gasped as he dragged his tongue up her opening. Moving to her swollen belly, he pressed his lips to her belly button and blew until she giggled, then laughed, then snorted.

'Mock!' She grabbed at his head but he thrust away and seized her wrists, pinning them to the ground. Getting to his knees, he straddled her. His eyes gleamed into hers. His hair trailed in a messy wave down his broad shoulders. His cock, already slightly hardened again, lay soft and sticky against her belly.

Grinda's heart thundered. 'What are you going to do with me?'

He whipped the hair out of his face. 'That would be up to you. We can do it the easy way or the hard way.' His eyes dropped to her breasts and Grinda watched as the soft skin of his cock hardened to a shine. When he raised his eyes again, they were dark with hunger. He licked his lips.

His hair fell back around his face as he leaned over and kissed her so passionately it lit a second fire between her legs. She smiled against his lips.

The easy way and the hard way.

Both.

# She-wolf

'It's beautiful, *bial*, and so warm!'

Grinda rubbed her arms up and down the sleeves of her *brinta*: a long-sleeved tunic made of tanned hide with fleece on the inside. It was big enough that it stretched over her belly and had plenty of room for growth. It felt so good against her skin. She smoothed her hands down the legs of her new britches. They were made the same way. She'd never been so warm.

'Of course, *biala*,' Mock kissed her on the lips, 'only the best for you. I'm only sorry it took so long.'

She shook her head, unable to believe he could make something so wonderful. It was made from the hide of a strange ram that wandered the forests. He'd caught one, killed it and carefully skinned it, then spent the last several days sewing in the fleece and tanning the hide. She wrapped her arms around herself. He had put so much love and care into it, it almost felt like she was carrying him along with her, as though the *brinta* was his arms wrapped lovingly around her. She pressed her nose to the material and took a breath. It almost smelled like him.

Meanwhile, Mock still wore only his *kinta*. He didn't seem to feel the cold. It was strange. Not that Grinda minded. There was nothing she liked better than raking her eyes down his strong, hard body. Seemingly of their own will, her eyes dropped to his navel, where she followed his trail of hair down to the top of his *kinta*.

'Come, *biala*.' He took her hand and smiled at her in a way that suggested he knew exactly what she was thinking. 'Time to move on.'

The forests had noticeably thickened the further north they journeyed, but they weren't yet close to the grandness of the forests of his people, so Mock said.

'The trees are so tall that you can crane your neck right back and still not see into their highest branches .... the water is as sweet as wine ... the wind is warm and filled with the scent of *lillas* ... the colours ... the soft earth ... you're going to love it, *biala*.'

He was exaggerating, of course: reality was rarely like one remembered. Still, she'd never seen him so wistful. It was strange to think how disgusted he had once been at the idea of going home. Now ...

When he looked at her, his eyes bright, his lips pulled back into that sweet smile he reserved only for her, she could see their future shining in his eyes: their love, their children. It made her curl into him and grip him tight. She no longer had fear for their future. No matter how the Quarthi might treat her, she had Mock and he would always love and protect her.

They set up camp deep in the woods. Mock lit a small fire but Grinda no longer needed its warmth. It did push the darkness away, however, and she was grateful for that. Mock might be excited about the woods but she was yet to get used to the sheer quiet and blackness. It could get so dark between the trees you could hardly see anything at all.

'Have no fear, *biala,* I am with you.' Pushing aside her hair, he kissed the back of her neck. He always seemed to know what she was feeling.

She gripped onto Mock's arms at the sound of a howl. Another howl followed. Then a third. Winter stomped his hoof, snorting in fear.

Mock wrapped his arms around her. 'They are far away, and wolves rarely eat men.' He kissed her again. 'Like I said, have no fear, I will protect you.'

She nodded but his words didn't ease the chill creeping up her spine.

*

Later that night, Mock left the tent, his belt of knives already strapped to his waist, his sword tight in his fist.

Wolves.

They had come, after all. Quietly, he untied Winter and dragged him over to the tent where he tied him to another tree, nice and close. He could let the wolves take the old horse down if he had to, giving him and Grinda a chance to escape, but he really didn't want to. Grinda was getting big and was finding it hard to walk. They needed the beast, old and slow though he might be.

Next, he woke Grinda.

'What is it?' she said in the darkness. She was sleeping deep under the pelts.

'Just come. We are in danger. I need you out of the tent.'

She looked at his sword, about to ask another question, when she froze at a growl. Winter whinnied. His hooves thudded. The horse had never been so full of life—or fear.

Instinctively, Mock grabbed at his belt. He didn't need to say anything more. Grinda staggered to her feet. She was trembling as Mock took her arm.

It was dark between the trees, the sky thick with clouds, but he could hear well enough. That growl again, deeper, closer. Grinda sucked in a breath at a second growl. Mock pushed her behind him, still gripping her arm. They turned at another growl. He could feel Grinda's warm, frightened breaths against his back. She grabbed his hip, fingers digging in around the bone. Then the wolves revealed themselves, one by one, all three of them, little more than shadows, except for the gleam of an eye or a canine. Two were dark, one grey. More growling, the licking of chops. Then they began to circle.

Winter screamed, then reared, his hooves thudding heavily against the ground. He shook his head, wrenching hard at his reins. It did nothing to break the wolves' focus. Mock could see their intent: they wanted the horse, first and foremost. Man-meat was secondary.

Mock tightened his grip on Grinda's arm and slowly backed away. He would leave them to it.

'No,' Grinda said.

Mock paused.

'*Grinda.*'

'No. I will not leave him.'

Grinda tried to push past him.

He pushed back. 'What are you doing?'

'Trust me.'

She tried again but he wouldn't let her pass.

One of the black wolves snarled. Its face lit up as a cloud passed over the moon and Mock saw that it was female, skinny, with long heavy teats that dangled beneath her belly. Her lips were drawn back, the hackles raised on her neck.

Mock shivered at a strange tickling sensation that seemed to itch at his brain. All three wolves stiffened. The grey one lifted its head. The dark male licked his chops. The female stared. They all stared—at Grinda. And suddenly Mock understood what she was doing.

Mind Speak.

'They're just hungry, Mock.'

'What does it matter? I won't let us be their prey.'

She tore her arm out of his grip and shoved past, and this time Mock didn't try to pull her back. She stood in front of Mock—protecting *him*—all five feet of her. Clenching her hands at her sides, she lifted her chin. Mock tightened his grip on his sword.

Winter reared again but quietly now, snorting and grunting. His big panting breaths came out in puffs of white mist.

Again, that itch. Mock cricked his neck.

The large dark male ducked his head, gave a low growl, then began to back away. The grey followed. The female lingered. She stared at them with her silvery eyes, then sat, panting. She licked her chops and whined.

'Go,' Grinda said. 'Leave us.'

The she-wolf whined again, stood, then turned and hurried away. Mock didn't move, still gripping his sword.

'I'm cold, Mock.'

He scoured the surrounding trees. 'Just wait. They could come back.'

Grinda gripped her arms. 'They won't come back.'

'How can you be sure?' She frowned at him. He lowered his sword. 'All right, *biala*. Go back in but I'm going to stay out here a little while longer.'

'As you wish.' Standing on her tiptoes, she kissed him on the lips.

She crawled back inside.

Mock stood guard until dawn, but the wolves didn't return.

*

'You sure she's here?'

'Definitely.' Grinda looked around the trees. *And she's watching us.*

Mock dropped the deer leg, adding it to the rest of the carcass he'd quartered. He stretched himself out with a low moan, pushing out his chest as he cricked his neck. Grinda watched him with a crooked smile.

Mock smiled back. 'You sure about this, *biala*?'

'Definitely.' She turned to look at the surrounding woods. 'I promised her.'

Taking her hand, he kissed it. 'Then come. Let's not push her patience.'

They hid a short distance away, lying low against the ground. They waited a long time, hearing only the rustling of bushes and the creaking of branches. Mock was stiff beside her. She could almost feel his disbelief.

A while later, when they still hadn't appeared, she began to doubt herself too. She and Mock kept their distance, out of sight of the waiting carcass, but close enough they would hear their approach.

And hear them they finally did.

There was a sharp yap, then quiet again. Then more sharp yapping. Grinda glanced at Mock, who looked at her in surprise. Grinda could sense them as well as hear them: the two males, the starving she-wolf and her litter of six. They all approached. The two males stood guard, panting, their tongues lolling. The mother was cautious, keeping her young back, sensing Mock and Grinda's presence.

Grinda tried to ease her worries. *Trust. Yours.*

Again, the she-wolf hesitated, but her pups were starving. Grinda could feel their little hearts galloping and their stomachs churning as they smelled the blood.

*Eat*

Finally, the she-wolf relented. Mock laughed at the sound of the pups' rapturous yapping as they took their fill of the carcass. Grinda took his hand and squeezed.

Mock smiled at her proudly. 'This is a good thing, *biala*. The Mother will be pleased.'

Grinda smiled.

They both turned back to the family of wolves, side by side, hand in hand, as they listened to their joy.

# Past & Future

'Mmm. That's nice, *biala*.'

Chuckling, Grinda continued to drag her fingers through his hair. It was so thick, much thicker than hers. And so coarse! Though that might have more to do with the fact he never brushed it. She loved it either way.

They had stopped for lunch and the sun sat high in the sky, glinting brightly. It almost made his hair gleam a deep red, his skin too. She was kneeling in soft grass behind him, his smooth broad back and his hard shoulders beneath her hands. No more scars. No more pain. She massaged him a moment, trying to dig in her knuckles where she knew his knots lay, but it was useless: his muscles were just too big. She usually had to walk on him, digging in her heels.

She kissed the nape of his neck, smiling as he shivered. His hair was starting to shine now, her fingers moving smoothly through his locks. Back at Quay she had never had anyone she could braid hair with: no sister, or friend who hadn't been busy; and her mother had scoffed at the suggestion. Never in her wildest dreams would she have thought that she would one day be playing with the hair of her barbarian lover.

Hair that gleamed as beautiful as any maiden's.

Grinda chuckled again.

'What are you laughing at?'

'Nothing.' She raised herself higher on her knees as she began on his fringe, pulling it into a tight plait.

'Don't make me look too pretty,' he said, only half-jokingly. 'If we meet anyone on our way, I need to be taken seriously.'

'Isn't that a good thing? Isn't that what you've always said to me? That it's best for your enemy to underestimate you?'

'For a woman, yes, but not for a man.'

She continued, his hair weaving easily through her fingers. Then she was done; two long braids on either side. He certainly looked pretty from the back.

'All right. Turn around.'

He did. Grinda pursed her lips, trying not to laugh. He twisted his mouth as he peered down at his braids, fondling them between his thick, strong fingers. Grinda couldn't take it anymore. Slapping a hand to her mouth, she burst out laughing.

Mock kept his face straight but his eyes were shining.

She squealed as he tackled her, pinning her to the ground between his thighs. She squealed again, turning away as he began flicking his braids in her face.

'Stop!' she screamed with laughter. 'They hurt!'

He laughed, then pressed his mouth to hers. She closed her eyes, quiet, as he stretched out on top of her, sucking her tongue. Then she opened them again and the laughter returned.

She spluttered against his lips. 'St-st-stop! I can't do it. You look funny.'

He tugged at his right braid. 'Mmm. I don't know. They're growing on me. Maybe you could do my beard too.'

Leaning over, he blew his lips against her neck. She thrust him away with a snort, throwing him onto his back. He stretched out under the sun. His *kinta* had hoisted right up, revealing the wrinkled bottom of his balls. Now it was Grinda who was straddling him. Mock gripped her hips, grinning up at her, as she began to unwind his braids.

It seemed to take forever, and by the time she was done, her mouth was all over his mouth, his jaw, his throat. The sun was burning against her head and the back of her neck but she couldn't care: she had Mock right where she wanted him.

She reached beneath his *kinta*, smoothing her hand up his hardened length. Mock closed his eyes with a groan.

\*

Afterwards, Mock lay spent beside her. She was breathing deeply, curled up against his chest, as he traced his fingers up and down her back. He would never forget how he felt the first time he'd seen her bare back; how beautiful it had been. She had been trembling against him, fearful and hateful. He still couldn't believe how far they had come. How far *he* had come since his days as Mock the Merciless: leader of his raiding brothers, murderer, fiend and rapist.

Just look at him now.

Far from filling him with regret, it made his heart swell. Slowly, Mock ran his hand up along the length of her naked body. She was so soft. It amazed him that he'd once thought to kill her.

Careful not to wake her, he kissed her gently on the head, then eased out of her arms. She murmured in her sleep, curling into a ball in the cold. Mock fetched their pelts and laid them over her.

The sun had set hours before and the moon sat like a giant orb high in the sky. It was so bright its light engulfed the twinkling of the stars. It turned the landscape white and blazed against Winter's coat. The horse almost gleamed.

Standing beside the old beast, Mock slung his arm over his neck. They'd made camp at the top of a hill, and the forest spread out below them in an ocean of rippling leaves. The sight of it made his heart soar. He couldn't be further away from the cold, hard cells of Fairmont. His back itched as he remembered the old tortures. On the surface the scars were healed but he still bore their marks deep beneath.

Not even the Mother could heal those.

His stomach twisted. How long before all this would be gone—he couldn't predict. And what about his people? Each generation the Quarthi were forced to retreat further and further from the Paleskins. How long before they were backed up against the ocean, with nowhere else to go?

It was only a matter of time. The end was drawing near.

He looked back at Grinda, and his dark thoughts dispersed. Whatever may come, he would relish the time he had. There was no point in agonising over the future, not when there was so much yet to be enjoyed.

He returned. Lifting the pelts, he eased back in beside her. She stirred, her eyes opening a crack.

'Sorry,' he whispered, kissing her on the lips.

Grinda smiled, kissing him lightly back. 'You can wake me any time, *bial*.' Her eyes opened wider. She touched his cheek. 'You're sad.'

'No.'

'Liar.'

He smiled. 'Just thinking.'

'Then stop thinking.'

She kissed him again, this time passionately. Mock opened his mouth, letting her in. They were quiet a long time. A bird called from the branches of a nearby tree. Winter snorted. The breeze made the grass rustle.

But soon all that disappeared and all he heard were Grinda's panting breaths, her little grunts, the wet sucking as he thrust into her. She gave a little cry. He grunted. A gush. Warmth. Wetness. His heart pounded hard in his chest.

An empty mind, a swollen heart and a pair of blue eyes that filled the night even more brightly than the blazing moon.

'Mock,' she whispered.

'Grinda,' he murmured.

They pressed their cheeks together, arms wrapped around each other so tightly there was no space between them. Their hearts pounded. They breathed each other's breaths. She gave a surprised grunt as he moved inside her. He pushed deeper, harder, wanting to feel her, to know her.

Inside as well as out.

'Still sad?' Grinda murmured in his ear.

Mock threaded his fingers through her hair, enjoying how the moonlight made it glimmer and gleam. 'Was I sad?'

Grinda smiled. Mock smiled. He kissed her jaw, then her throat, before slumping against her with a sigh.

Sad, happy, content—sometimes it was hard to tell the difference.

# Zin

*29 weeks pregnant*

'Are you all right, Grinda?'

Catching her tongue between her teeth, Grinda shifted awkwardly on Winter's back. She glanced at Mock who'd already dismounted, then looked at the ground. Was the horse getting taller? He'd never seemed so high. She tried to lift one of her legs to swing herself off but her courage failed her, and she gripped onto his white mane helplessly. At twenty-nine weeks she was so big and unwieldy that the smallest things cost the biggest effort.

'I think I'm stuck.' She felt her face flush.

Mock laughed. 'Understandable.' Resting his hand on Winter's neck, he looked up at her. 'Let me help you.'

'Don't hurt yourself, Mock. I'm heavy now.'

His voice was gentle. 'Not for me, *biala*.'

She bit her lip but reached for him. His strength always amazed her. He was quick. Before she had time to help, he'd dragged her from the horse's back and into his arms. He stood there for a moment, cradling her, his eyes dark and soft. 'See. As light as air.'

He lowered her to her feet.

Grinda stretched with a groan as Mock secured Winter. Her neck, her back, her legs—everything ached. She smoothed her hands over her belly. So big now. Too big. She could no longer see her toes. It was getting hard to sit down, to stand up, to lie on her back.

The rides were getting shorter too. Only rarely did she ask to stop, trying not to complain or seem weak, but Mock always paid close attention to how she was feeling and always seemed to know when she'd had enough. He was never impatient or frustrated, though his people's forest was still far into the distance and the birth was rapidly approaching.

When he turned to the supplies at the beast's back, Grinda went to help.

'No, *biala*. You go rest. I can set up camp on my own.'

'I'm not useless, Mock.'

His mouth twisted as he tried not to smile. 'If you say so.' He removed the deer-hide tent and handed it over. 'Here then. Go lay it out and I'll join you.'

It was tied up in a slim roll. It was heavy, but she clutched it with both arms to her chest. It was only mid-afternoon; they could have ridden for hours more yet. But Grinda was too tired and sore to argue.

Finding a small level spot of land between the trees, she bent to lay the tent on the ground, only to stop partway. She couldn't do it! She couldn't bend over! She attempted to crouch, only to regret it.

'Something wrong?' Mock said from behind.

Grinda sighed. 'I think you'd better do it.' She handed the tent over.

Mock took it with a small, sultry smile.

Grinda sat comfortably with her back up against a tree as she watched him work. His hair was loose and knotted, any memory of the braids long gone. It draped his face in a dark curtain every time he bent over. Then he'd push it back, revealing the strong cording of his neck and the hard muscles of his shoulders.

He had a lot of muscles in his back too and she watched as they rolled under his skin. She clenched her hands, recalling their hard smoothness against her palms. She dragged her eyes down the length of his spine, from the broad power of his shoulders, to the narrow hard core of his lower back and the top of his *kinta*.

Then there were those strong legs and round arse.

He was quick with his work, and was soon hammering the pins into the earth, his arms bulging at every hit, the veins of his forearms thick and ropey. Every time he lifted his arm, she could see the soft hair of his armpit and the muscles bunched up along his side. And then she'd see his face, that small smile, those soft eyes—so content, as though he were enjoying every minute of it.

Grinda stood as he finished hammering in the last of the pins. Before he rose, Grinda placed her hands against his shoulders, thumbs pressing lightly into the thick muscles around his neck.

She kissed the back of his head. 'Thank you, *bial*,' she said huskily.

He slowly straightened from his crouch, towering over her. Smiling, he gently took her face and kissed her slow and deep.

\*

They sat outside: Grinda in Mock's lap, Mock's back up against a tree. The fire flickered, chasing away the shadows. They didn't speak for a long time, simply holding each other. Her back was warm against his chest. His heart beat against her back. It was often like this: no words to say, only sensation and the feeling of contentment that so often seemed to surround them both in a warm bubble.

No cares. No worries. Long blissful days stretched out into the distance.

Mock had his chin on her head, his hands around her belly, as he felt the usually soft but sometimes hard kicks of his daughter. His eyes were closed, his shoulders relaxed. He kissed Grinda's head. His heart felt so swollen it seemed to fill the whole of his chest and reach into his throat.

He floated. He soared.

Grinda gasped at a sudden hard kick. Mock chuckled. Grinda gripped onto his hand.

'She's going to be a fighter,' he said.

'I hope so.'

'She'll be a great hunter. I'll make sure of it. A great warrior too.'

Grinda turned to look at him, eyes bright and wide. 'Your women can be warriors?'

'Of course.'

'But how?'

'There's more to fighting and hunting than just strength: speed, stamina, skill, instinct, focus. A good warrior uses their brain.' He smoothed his hands over her belly. 'A lot of male warriors forget that, relying too heavily on their strength. That's why they're so often defeated.'

Grinda shook her head in disbelief, then turned back to the forest, silent and thoughtful. An owl hooted. Something rustled through the undergrowth. A cool breeze made the fire flicker, throwing a dance of light and shadow against the trees.

'Thought of a name for her yet?' Mock finally said.

'I've tried,' she shrugged, 'but nothing seems right. Though it's a beautiful name, Mirabelle or the like just wouldn't fit. She needs something ...'

'... stronger,' they both finished.

Mock brushed the hair away from the back of her neck. 'Have you considered using a name from my people?'

She turned to look at him again. 'You have an idea?'

'Several.'

'Tell them to me.'

He smiled as he dragged his finger across her lips, then lowered his eyes to her belly. Her hand rested against it. Her *brinta* was stretched tight.

'Vex: Light and darkness. The in between. The shadows that swallow the light. The light that eats the shadows.

'Drinn: The deepest oceans. The highest heights. The blackest night. The unknown beyond.

'Pax: Stepping stones, paths and journeys. Into the horizon.

'Zin: Sun and moon. Fire and gleaming water. The light that never fades.'

'The light that never fades,' Grinda repeated, tapping her lips. Her face brightened, then softened. 'Zin.' She looked down at her belly. 'My sun and moon. Zin.' She looked up at him.

'It's your choice, Grinda.'

She shook her head. 'No. She's your daughter too.'

He laid his hand against her belly. 'It's a good name. A strong name.' Particularly if what he'd seen beyond the ether was true—those black eyes. She would need all the light she could get.

Grinda was watching him. He wiped the thought from his mind and smiled. 'Zin. My daughter. May you grow big and strong and brave, and know only light and happiness for all your days.' Lowering his head, he kissed Grinda's navel. When he sat back up, Grinda's eyes were glittering.

She took his hand and squeezed it. 'It's beautiful. Thank you, *bial.*'

He smiled, brushed the hair out of her eyes, then kissed her.

Grinda lay against his chest with a sigh, Mock's hand still on her belly, on his daughter. He smoothed his hands over her, over them both.

Zin: the light that never fades.

# Family

M ock twisted his mouth, trying very hard not to laugh.

'Ink dot perthi,' Grinda said.

How he tried. But the laughter burst from his lips, echoing through the forest.

Grinda punched him hard in the shoulder. Or, at least, *she* thought it was hard.

He looked down at the red mark she'd left behind. 'What's that? A fleabite?'

She gave him a light-hearted scowl. 'I'm trying my best.'

'I know you are, and I appreciate it.' And it was cute: those little frown lines between her eyes as she concentrated. 'Learning another language is hard. I should know.'

'How long did it take for you to learn?'

'A few months.'

Her blue eyes widened. 'Months? But I know almost nothing and we've been together almost ten!'

'True. But you didn't have a whip at your back to give you incentive.'

She frowned, then kissed him on the fading red mark. 'I'm sorry.'

He sighed. 'Stop apologising. You're not the one who tortured me. Now, try again. And this time—' he leaned in toward her and gently took her chin '—roll your tongue.'

Taking a breath, she closed her eyes and tried again.

'Better.' He kissed her on the lips.

'But not perfect.'

Mock slung an arm around her shoulders. 'Give yourself time, *biala*. You'll get it. Once you're with my people, you'll learn quickly.'

They both gazed through the trees. They were getting close now, Mock could feel it: all those old smells and sensations. It made his heart swell and plummet at the same time. So many fond and terrible memories.

'You're thinking about her, aren't you?'

Her name whispered through the trees. *Danna.*

Mock frowned. 'I try not to. But this place ...' Shaking his head, he raised his eyes to the canopy where the bright noonday light made the leaves glow.

Grinda pressed in close. 'Think about her all you like, Mock. She's a part of you.'

'As you're a part of me, *biala*.' He kissed her on the head. 'But I'd rather think of the future.'

He felt her smile against him as she stroked the hairs on his chest. 'And what do you think about?'

'Our children.'

Grinda looked up at him. 'I think about them too, so much. Already, they make me so happy and they're not even born.' She pinched the brown skin at his waist. 'I wonder what they'll look like: half-Toth, half-Quarthi.'

'They'll look like you, Grinda. I imagine seeing you in all their faces.'

'No,' she frowned. 'I want them to look like you. I don't want them to be different to your people.'

'My people will get what they get. I don't care what they think.'

'But our children might.'

He frowned down at her. 'Our lives will be happy. I'll make it so.' He clenched his fist around his knee. 'And I dare anyone to threaten that.'

Grinda smoothed her hand along his chest. 'How many?'

'How many what?'

'How many children do you want?'

'Ten.'

Grinda laughed.

'I want the forest filled with their laughter,' Mock continued. 'I want the clan terrorised by their troublemaking. I want to be exhausted and sleepless. I want to have my hands so full, my heart so swollen, my mind so tired that all I can think about is my future and their future and your future and nothing of the terrors of the past.

'I want to know what it's like to hold my sons in my arms, and my daughters. I want them to run to me when they're sad, hug me when they're scared, laugh and play with me.' He pulled Grinda close, wrapping his arms around her as he stared into her eyes. 'You don't know how much.'

Grinda stared back, her eyes shining with tears. 'I think I might.' She brushed her fingers through his beard. 'Ten children, then. Well, Zin will be born soon. It seems we've got a lot of work to do in the coming months.'

Mock pressed his lips to hers. 'I wouldn't call it work, *biala*.'

*

Grinda kissed him back. Ten children. He was exaggerating, of course, but the thought didn't frighten her. The world could only get better with a few more Mocks running around.

She kissed him harder as he slowly dragged up her *brinta*. Her breasts were so swollen now they ached every time she moved and even when she didn't. Hoisting the *brinta* up over them, Mock stopped to stare. His eyes were dark as he held them both in his big hands. A bead of milk glistened on her left nipple. He stroked it away, then pressed his mouth there. She gasped, arching her neck. She'd never been so sensitive.

He pulled back, licking his lips, then kissed her on the mouth again. His hands lowered to her backside, one long finger stroking her lightly along her crack until she shivered. He slipped down her britches. Then his hand was between her legs, stroking softly. Like her breasts, her groin was hypersensitive too. His finger almost seemed to burn against her skin. Then it penetrated, deeply, slowly, and it was as though her whole body was boiling over.

She felt the heat fill her cheeks. 'Mock,' she gasped.

He dragged her into his lap, their hot groins pressed against each other, her swollen breasts pressed up against his hard chest. Kissing. Panting. Sucking. Moisture trickled down the inside of her thigh and Grinda couldn't tell whether it was from him or from her.

Seizing her waist, he lifted her with his massive strength, his face twisted and strained as he tried to keep control of himself. His hard cock pressed between her legs. Grinda grabbed a hold of it, directing it inside herself as he slowly lowered her over him.

She gritted her teeth. It seemed to take forever, and he seemed to swell bigger and bigger the more he entered her. Slowly. Almost painfully. Then it was done, and she was back in his lap.

Mock was panting. Grinda was gasping. His eyes were so dark they were almost black, his lashes thick and sooty. Coiling her fingers in his beard, she kissed him on the lips. Closing his eyes, he kissed her softly back. How he could be so ravenous one moment and so tender the next never stopped surprising her.

Opening his eyes, he pressed his forehead to hers. They didn't move for a long time, simply enjoying being a part of each other. The forest disappeared and her worries along with it.

Ten children.

It didn't seem so far-fetched anymore. He stroked her cheek. She stroked his. Then they were moving. And it was as though the world was rocking along with them. His arms tightened around her shoulders. Her arms tightened around his waist. Tighter and tighter they squeezed. Faster and faster they rocked. His beard brushed against her ear as she pressed her face into the corner of his jaw.

Then it was over. Mock shuddered inside her. Grinda sucked in a breath. The forest slowly returned. The world stopped rocking. Then there was just their panting breaths and their pounding hearts.

She kissed his throat. He kissed her shoulder. Slowly, they pulled back, still holding each other, still united. The darkness had faded from his eyes. They were pink now, his smile relaxed. Brushing his fingers gently through her fringe, he kissed her on the nose.

His cock slipped out of her. She felt the hot wetness of his seed running down her thigh, and she couldn't help but think what a waste it was: a potential child, something more to love.

She dragged her hand down his chest. 'You're right, *bial*.'

'Right about what?' he breathed.

She smiled, then kissed him, murmuring against his lips, 'I wouldn't call it work.'

# The Quarthi

Mock was tense. Grinda could feel it in the hardness of his waist beneath her hands and see it in the stiffness in his shoulders. Winter felt it too, his ears flicking everywhere as he nickered nervously.

The forest was so thick here she couldn't see the sky, only a thin trickle of ruddy light through the canopy. Mock had hoped to arrive before sunset. He got his wish. Though Grinda ached all over: in her heavy breasts, in her lower back, her legs and groin, she didn't complain, making the four-hour journey by gritting her teeth.

Now, she was too tired to be fearful.

At the sound of a bird call, Mock turned his head. Grinda stiffened. Winter's ears flicked towards the left. Another bird call echoed the first from the opposite side.

They were surrounded.

'Stay on Winter,' Mock had told her before they'd begun their journey that afternoon. 'No matter what. If I get off or should fall or anything happens to me, you ride back as far and as fast as you can.'

'You think they might hurt us?'

'I don't know. I've been gone too long. I have no idea what's happened to them since. I can't even be sure of their location.'

But the location was right, and Grinda couldn't believe she was actually here.

'I am Mock,' he called in Quarthi into the trees, turning Winter as he did, his hands tight around the reins. He spoke more Quarthi words Grinda struggled to understand. He spoke about her, their child and something about escape and return.

'Mock,' came a voice.

Their heads turned.

'Kopta,' Mock replied in surprise. He said something more in Quarthi. Grinda recognised the word *friend* but that was all.

Grinda dared to peer around Mock's broad back, squinting into the forest. The Quarthi man blended so well with one of the thick trunks of the trees her eyes passed over him several times before she saw him.

He looked remarkably like Mock in so many ways: bronze skin, thick dark hair tied into a tail, broad jawline. But he lacked Mock's height and size and looked several years older.

'Kopta' approached and Grinda tightened her grip around Mock's waist.

Mock turned to look at her. 'Have no fear, *biala*. He's an old friend of mine.'

Dismounting, Mock gave her the reins. The two men kept a wary distance from each other as they spoke. Grinda lifted her eyes to the rest of the forest, and that was when she saw the others, many others, at least half a dozen. Her pulse began to race. Mostly men, some women, all armed with spears or bows. All wore the same belts as Mock did, though the knives were different, made of bone, not steel.

Four of them were staring at her. No, not staring, *glaring* at her. A tingle rushed down her spine. One had her arrow nocked and was aiming straight at her head.

She was about to call out to Mock when laughter boomed around the clearing. Mock and Kopta were grinning at each other as they grasped forearms in what Grinda had come to know was their 'warrior's grip'. They then turned away from each other: Kopta returned to the trees and Mock returned to Grinda.

'It's all right, *biala*.' He took the reins. 'They're going to lead us to the clan.'

Grinda wasn't so certain. She glanced towards the tree again but the woman with the bow was gone. 'Do you trust them?

His mouth thinned. 'As much as I can at this point.' He pressed his hand to her belly. 'The *shamri* already know of our coming. These warriors were sent out to wait for us. They know of Zin and they're ready for you. Everything is going to be fine.'

Grinda laid her hand on top of his. 'Truly?'

He grabbed her hand and squeezed. 'Truly.'

*

*Truly.*

The lie tasted foul in Mock's mouth, but what else should he say? He couldn't be certain of anything. Kopta was welcoming enough but he felt the wariness of the others, and why they should have come fully armed was troubling.

He tried to appear relaxed as he led Winter through the trees with Grinda mounted uncertainly on his back, but with his senses spanned out, his free hand close to the knives at his belt.

He heard the clan before he saw them, and to his surprise he felt his spirits lift. In spite of all the tragedy, these were the people he had grown up with. Children laughed and screamed. He could hear the shrill shouts of women, the bleating of a ram.

Looking up at Grinda, he smiled at her. Hand pressed to her belly, she smiled back. Before they broke through the trees and revealed themselves, Mock helped her down. Her hand was small in his but it gripped his tightly.

Side by side, they entered the clearing. The silence was almost instant: heads turned, conversation stopped, even the screaming children quietened. Then a familiar voice cracked through the silence like a whip. 'Mock! Grinda!'

Mock grinned. Grinda cried out desperately. 'Croki!'

The big Quarthi warrior didn't seem to notice the reaction of the clan as he marched over and gripped Mock's arm, pulling him into a hug. Laughing, he slapped him on the back. 'My brother!' His eyes softened as they lowered to Grinda. 'And sister. Ye gettin' big!' Grinda's welcome was much more reserved: a swift, one-armed embrace. Clearly, he hadn't forgotten Mock's warning from their last meeting.

'Croki, I've missed you,' Grinda said, grinning widely.

'Missed you too. Come! I've got some deer on the fire.'

Mock led over Winter and tied him securely. A large ram with an enormous pair of testicles eyed the old horse warily, almost as warily as the clan eyed Mock and Grinda. They kept their distance but surrounded them in a loose circle, watching shamelessly.

The men and women muttered to each other but the children weren't so discreet, tugging at their parents' hands, hissing *faqwa* under their breath so loudly they might as well have been shouting it.

Mock kept Grinda close, his arm tight around her waist. 'Don't be nervous.' He leaned down and kissed her on the lips in front of them all, then placed his hand on her belly. If his people entertained any doubt about their relationship, they had none now.

Children gasped and giggled. There was a collective suck of breath. Muttering turned to grumbling.

Croki watched it all with a broad grin. 'Come and sit. Join us,' he told the Quarthi. 'The Paleskin won't bite, or are you afraid of a little woman?'

Nobody budged except to scowl or turn to leave. Several men and women skulked away. The rest twisted their mouths or grumbled.

Mock handed Grinda a hunk of deer flesh before taking some himself.

'Take the *faqwa* away!' an elder holding a staff suddenly exclaimed. 'She doesn't belong here and neither does the traitor.' He pointed a gnarled finger at Mock. Like the rest of the clan, he wore only his *kinta*. A nest of long, curly grey hair stood thick and matted on his chest and shoulders.

Grinda pressed up against Mock, face lowered. Mock spat out a chunk of gristle. 'If you weren't an elder, old man, I'd knock your head off. Remove yourself.' He glared at them all, most particularly at the young hunters and warriors, men and women both. A couple held spears. One had her hand at her belt of knives. 'And the rest of you. If you have a problem, go speak to the *shamri*. Or—' wiping his mouth, he stood '—you can tell me in private how much you want us gone.'

He pushed out his chest, parting his feet into a fighter's stance as he gripped the handle of one of his blades. One warrior with a long dark braid and an old scar across his chest looked ready to challenge him.

Then Croki stood, towering over Mock and the rest of them. Unlike Mock, he didn't care to hold back —unsheathing his own blade. 'You face him, you face me too.'

The fire in the warrior's eyes dimmed. The rest looked at each other with hard expressions. Nobody wanted to meet their challenge and fewer still wanted to speak with the *shamri*.

Steadily, they began moving away. Mock and Croki sat back down. Grinda hadn't taken a single bite of her deer meat. Grease and blood dripped down her wrist and into her lap.

'Eat, *biala.*'

She looked at him uncertainly.

'Have no fear, little *faqwa*, they'll come around,' Croki said gently.

She gave a sigh, then took a bite.

Croki and Mock looked at each other.

How long that would take only the Mother could know.

# The *Shamri*

Mock took Grinda's small, trembling hand in his.

'But they told me to come alone,' Grinda said.

'Not a chance, *biala*. Besides, they are the *shamri*, they should have foretold my coming.'

Grinda gave him a small smile and Mock kissed her on the head. The *shamri* lived apart from the rest of the clan. Not far, but it was a reminder of how different they were. It troubled her. It made her fear. If the general population of the Quarthi didn't trust her, then might not the *shamri* be worse?

She had been four days with the Quarthi and hadn't met one, and yet it almost felt like she knew them already. Both Mock and Croki hadn't held back with their warnings.

'They are powerful and all-knowing, little *faqwa*. When they ask questions, speak no half-truths and no full-lies, because it all will come to nothin'. They will know.'

'But be strong, *biala*. Try not to fear them or quail beneath their gaze. Remember, they might have power but so do you—more so. You are far greater than they. Most have not seen or done any of the remarkable things you have.'

Grinda had laid her hand over her belly. 'Most?'

'Only one has seen the world beyond the ether.'

*Thall*—the oldest and most powerful of the *shamri*. He was the one she needed to convince. He was the one who would make the final decision as to whether she could stay or not. Apparently over the last four days, he, as well as the others, had been watching her from afar with their mind vision.

Grinda took a deep breath, trying not to shiver at the thought of their wandering eyes. Mock tightened his grip on her hand. 'I will be with you, *biala*. At your side. They will harm you at their peril.'

They were following a well-worn path, the surrounding branches bent back out of the way, the earth hard beneath her feet. She looked above into the canopy. Moonlight glinted through the leaves. Somehow it made her calmer—the feel of so much life. Even after four days Grinda still couldn't get used to how magnificent the trees were, how large and old. And the *warks*—she could feel them. They were everywhere: far behind, far ahead, left and right. They were like little pockets of heat burning in her mind and heart. The one up ahead was like a raging fire, so close she could feel the thud of the mother's blood rushing through its roots and pounding in the earth like a heartbeat.

The trees pulled away as they stepped into a clearing.

And there the *shamri* were: six of them, mostly old, both men and women, waiting and watching. Their magic made the air tingle.

Her eyes swept over them briefly before latching onto the tree at their back—the *wark*. She took another breath but this time it wasn't out of fear, but surprise. Warmth, power—she felt it flood her veins.

Releasing Mock's hand, she stepped towards the group of seated witches, eyes finding the powerful *shamri* at the centre. *Thall.* He was big and broad but with a long white beard and grey hair, and skin that sagged off thinning muscle. Old knotted veins bulged along his arms and across his chest. Dark eyes. Heavy brow. Grinda flexed her fingers. She could feel the heat of him, his power. He almost drowned out the others.

Even still, he was nothing to Zin. The thought washed away the last of her fear, and Grinda lifted her chin.

'Well met Mock, Grinda.' An old woman nodded at them. Their eyes met, and a strange something seemed to flower in Grinda's mind: a name—Flip. Sixty-years-old, mother to three and grandmother to eight. She liked the warmth and hated the cold. A skilled fisherwoman but a poor hunter. Her favourite herb was *grinya*.

Flip's eyes widened as she realised Grinda was reading her thoughts. Realising the same, the rest of the *shamri* turned to each other, muttering, all except *shamri* Thall, who didn't move, continuing to stare at Grinda, dark-eyed and seemingly unsurprised. His eyes lowered to her belly.

Grinda dropped her hands to Zin protectively. 'I want to join your people. My daughter wants to join your people.'

Again, the *shamri* looked at each other, the murmuring and whispering becoming almost frantic.

'Quiet.' The old man's voice boomed around the clearing. 'Let her speak.' His wrinkled eyes lifted to hers again. He completely ignored Mock standing silently behind her. 'Why do you want to join the Quarthi?'

Grinda opened her mouth before suddenly realising she was speaking English while they were speaking Quarthi. And yet, somehow, they understood each other.

She closed her mouth. *For Mock. For my daughter.*

The silence that followed was worse than the frantic murmuring.

*And what about for yourself, faqwa?*

Grinda turned her eyes to a young man with hair that was almost black. He had a thin chest and a sharp, pointed beard. He held his mouth in a sneer.

*Will you renounce your god? Your ways?* another said, less aggressively but no less dismissively.

Grinda didn't bother to answer. Instead, she lifted her chin higher.

*You're more the fool to think she hasn't,* intervened the most powerful of them all.

Grinda turned back to Thall. His eyes seemed to bore into her eyes, into her thoughts, into her very soul. Again, she held back a shiver. What had he seen when he'd been watching her those four days from afar?

Good? Bad? Did he like her or hate her? Unlike the others, he kept his emotions to himself.

Slowly, he stood. He was much taller than she'd expected, as tall as Mock. Mock shifted uneasily behind her, then drew to her side.

The old *shamri* approached, dark eyes never leaving her face, except to glance again at her belly. Something cold passed over Grinda, then dissipated. Mock stepped in front of her.

The powerful *shamri* stopped. The others watched on.

'Watch yourself,' Mock told him.

'If I wanted to hurt her, I would have done so already.'

Mock didn't move. Grinda touched his hand. '*Mock.*'

He looked down at her, his brow all crinkled up. 'If you're sure, *biala.*' He stepped aside.

*Shamri* Thall stared at her. Grinda stood straight and tall, feet braced apart, refusing to drop her eyes. *He might be powerful but so am I. He might have seen the ether but so have I. I've brought a man back from the dead. I've seen the future. I know more about violence and fear and horror than he could ever know.*

If he heard her thoughts, he didn't show it.

Then, suddenly, his big broad hand was against her belly. Mock growled and grabbed the hilt of one of his knives. The air caught in Grinda's throat and she dropped her hands over the *shamri's*.

They stayed like that for a long time. She could feel the heat of him and smell his sweat. His hand was warm and calloused, his breathing deep and long. His expression didn't change, deep in thought, until he finally pulled away and there appeared a crease between his eyes.

Doubt? Fear? Concern?

Whatever it was, it wasn't good, and Grinda couldn't help but remember the darkness in her daughter's eyes down beyond the ether.

He went to move away when she seized his wrist. *What does it mean?*

He looked down at her gripping his wrist and she quickly released him.

*Can you do something?*

He didn't answer. Returning to the rest of the *shamri*, he sat back down.

Giving an offhanded wave, he said, 'Welcome to the clan. May you and yours enjoy the warmth of the Mother's love.'

Two of the *shamri*, particularly the man with the pointed beard, shifted angrily.

'Th-thank you,' Grinda said, taken aback. It was that easy? No questions? No interrogation? She looked up at Mock. His eyes were narrowed and he was frowning.

They were both quiet on the way back, the air between them thick with disbelief. His hand was warm and strong in hers. The forest seemed to close in around her like a warm blanket, safe and protective. And slowly, the excitement cracked through her unease.

'What are you thinking, Mock?'

He squeezed her hand. 'Same thoughts you are, *biala.*'

She rubbed at her belly and smiled. By the time she returned to camp she couldn't stop grinning. Croki took one look at her and leapt to his feet with a triumphant roar. Forgetting all about their awkward past, he pulled her into a tight hug, hoisting her off her feet.

'Knew ye'd do it!' He slapped Mock on the back. 'Welcome to the clan!'

Grinda glanced at the rest of the Quarthi. They weren't so welcoming, but it was a beginning.

It was a beginning.

# Birth

In her mind she had always known it would hurt. After all, she'd been there at the birth of numerous babies back at her village, including her little brothers. But her mind was one thing, reality was something entirely different.

She tried not to scream. She'd been told Quarthi women didn't scream, but she wasn't Quarthi and with all this pain, they had to be lying. At another wave of agony, the scream poured from her lips whether she wanted it to or not, shattering the quiet of the forest. She rocked on her hands as the *shamri* busied around her backside. It was very undignified. The women of Toth always gave birth on their backs, though that seemed hardly better right now.

'It will be easier on the baby and on you,' the *shamri* had told her. 'All mothers give birth upright, whether beast or human.'

*Beast. Upright.* She rocked harder at another ripping cramp. Apparently, many Quarthi women bore their children standing up. That would never happen. She was no hero. Hands and knees would do—like an animal.

A warm hand pressed against her shoulder; a gentle voice spoke in her ear. '*Biala*, it's not too late.'

Grinda shook her head, sweat flinging in all directions from her sopping hair. 'No. I can do this.'

She might scream and she might kneel but she wouldn't take their drug. No *chokra*. It might ease the pain but it would damage her image, not that she had much of an image yet. The Quarthi were not impressed with her. She'd only been a part of the clan one month and had a lot to prove. *Chokra* was a weakness too far, a failure as a woman, as a mother and as a Quarthi. No Quarthi woman had ever taken the drug unless she was dying, no matter how many hours labour or how the child might rip her insides out.

She sat up on her knees, and Mock helped steady her as she swayed. Her belly was huge, bigger than she'd ever seen on any woman. The Quarthi natives were so much larger than her own people. It wasn't surprising that her baby—half Toth, half Quarthi—was just as big.

Another savage cramp and she screamed again. Mock knelt in front of her, his big warm hands on her shoulders. His eyes had sunken in, deep creases etched the corners of his mouth. Even despite the pain, it hurt to see him so worried. From somewhere outside of her agony she could hear the voices of the Quarthi women lift, followed by the noises of a sudden frenzied activity. Something was happening, but it was all so confusing and unimportant and far away. The pain, the exhaustion —that was all the world was now.

Then Mock pressed his forehead to hers, bringing her back. His eyes glittered. 'Breathe, *biala*, breathe. She is coming.'

Finally! She could have wept. Her cramping had started late-afternoon and now it was close to morning. Sweat trickled between her breasts, down under her arms, behind her ears. She hadn't eaten, hadn't drunk, hadn't even passed water. The world spun.

But she was coming!

Mock seized onto her at another convulsion, wrapping his arms around her as she cried out. A second convulsion. Another wave of agony. Her hips seemed to twist. Something seemed to split inside her. There was a rush of heat, a searing agony between her legs, then something finally gave.

She felt a gush, and Grinda widened her legs as Zin began to slide out of her: slippery, hard and huge. She opened her legs more, gripping onto Mock harder as her opening widened to a point she couldn't believe.

Another gush, another wave of agony, a fast slippery slide, and she was out! Grinda sagged against Mock, trembling and gasping, no longer able to hold herself up. Mock kissed her cheek, her neck, her shoulder, then embraced her as he rocked her from side to side. 'You did it, *biala*.'

Her heart thundered. She gasped for breath. The Quarthi women were doing things to her. Vaguely, she could feel their hands against her backside and between her legs, gabbling to each other as they worked. Then there was a sudden wail, one that twisted her insides and made her heart lurch. Pulling away from Mock, she turned, and that lurch turned to something that swelled, so big she thought her heart would burst.

*My baby. My daughter.*

Grinda must have been crying; hot tears spilled down her cheeks. She held her hands out and suddenly she was there, in her arms, a small pink bundle, a brown thatch on her head, mouth wide as she continued to wail. But then Grinda pressed her against her breasts and that wide, beautiful mouth stopped its screaming.

Silent. Content. Happy in her mother's arms.

And that was when everything disappeared: all the noise, the forest, the ground beneath her. Even Mock. All except for that weight in her arms, that glimmer of light against that perfect, pink skin, that moist mouth against her breast. It didn't feel real.

The swelling didn't stop, and she wondered how her heart could withstand so much. Somehow she didn't feel so tired anymore. That half day of agony meant nothing.

In love again. For the second time.

How lucky was she?

A perfect little hand wrapped itself around Grinda's hair. Grinda smiled and it seemed to go on forever, stretching across her face, through the forest, spanning over lands and oceans and mountains until it enveloped the world.

'It's nice to meet you, little Zin.'

***

# The Slave

Book 2 of The Mother's Children

Almost twenty years have passed and Mock and Grinda's love has defied the odds. Their daughter Zin is now a grown woman. Born between two worlds—half Toth, half Quarthi—she finds herself isolated from the rest of the clan. What's more, she is surrounded by power and darkness—once firmly contained, now awakening. Not even the *shamri*, with all their magical might, can predict her future.

Lord Aaron is fourth in line to the throne. Ordered by his uncle to rid Toth of the last of the Quarthi, he draws together a force that will surely annihilate them. But he discovers Zin—startling and unexpected—and something begins to change in his heart.

Then there's the Darkness. The *Morgrar*. Insidiously creeping into their world. Only united can the Toths and the Quarthi hope to defeat it. Will they join forces before it's too late?

# The Darkness

Book 3 of The Mother's Children

Zin has sacrificed herself to protect her land and her people, Quarthi and Toth alike. The Darkness has vanished. The Quarthi have their land back. The forest is regrowing.

Black Bull is part Quarthi, part Sand Person, black-skinned and strong; born a slave and trapped in the white city of Fairmont. When his mother's people demand the slaves' release, it is time for freedom. It is time to live his life. Will he find happiness with the savages or only more scorn and rejection?

Grinda and Mock grieve for Zin. With the help of the powerful *shamri* and Mock's unearthly connection, they discover something is consuming her from within. Something with a bottomless hunger to possess her. The *Morgrar* has not been destroyed, and it's up to those who love Zin to save her and return her to the light.

Mock will fight to the death. Grinda will never stop hoping. Aaron won't give up.

A dead world. Unlikely allegiances. An undying love.

The final chapter.

Made in the USA
Middletown, DE
17 June 2022